I DARE YOU

YOU

ILSA MADDEN-MILLS

Kim,
Thank You
so much!

Ilsa

Copyright © 2018 by Ilsa Madden-Mills
Cover Design by Shanoff Designs
Photography by Wander Aguiar
Editing by C Marie
Content Editing by Indie Girl Promotions
Ebook Formatting by Champagne Formats
Paperback Formatting by Shanoff Formats

Paperback
ISBN-13: 978-1986917964
ISBN-10: 1986917967

All rights reserved. Without limiting the rights under copyright reserved above, no part of this publication may be reproduced, stored in or introduced into a retrieval system, or transmitted in any form, or by any means (electronic, mechanical, photocopying, recording, or otherwise) without the prior written permission of the above copyright owner of this book or publisher.

This is a work of fiction. Names, characters, places, brands, media, and incidents are either the product of the author's imagination or are used fictitiously. The author acknowledges the trademarked statue and trademark owners of various products referenced in this work of fiction, which have been used without permission. The publication/use of these trademarks is not authorized, associated with, or sponsored by the trademark owners.

TABLE OF CONTENTS

DEDICATION

This book is for all the cool, smart girls in the world, especially the ones who love any of the following: hot football guys; cats; *Star Wars*; *The Princess Bride; He-Man; Sixteen Candles*; *The Goonies*; *Game of Thrones*; *Deadpool*; and, of course, it goes without saying…donuts, cookies, and pie.

From *Wall Street Journal* bestselling author Ilsa Madden-Mills comes a brand-new heartfelt, sexy contemporary romance about a smokin' hot football player and the good girl he falls for...

I DARE YOU

Badass Athlete: **I dare you to...**
Delaney Shaw: **Who is this?**

The late-night text is random, but "Badass Athlete" sure seems to know who she is...

Delaney Shaw.
Good girl.
Lover of fluffy kitties and Star Wars.
Curious.

His dare? Spend one night in his bed—a night he promises will be unforgettable—and she can solve the mystery of who he is.

She knows she shouldn't, but what else is she going to do with her boring Valentine's Day?

One sexy hook-up later, her mind is blown and the secret's out.

Maverick Monroe.
Bad boy.

The most talented college football player in the country. *Just ask him.*

Too bad for him Delaney's sworn off dating athletes forever after her last heartbreak.

But Maverick wants more than one night and refuses to give up on winning Delaney's heart. She isn't one to be fazed by a set of broad shoulders.

Will the bad boy land the nerd girl or will the secrets they keep from each other separate them forever?

I DARE YOU

PROLOGUE

FRESHMAN YEAR

DELANEY

Welcome to Magnolia, Mississippi, where locusts are as big as your hand and iced tea comes with a double helping of sugar.

It's also home to the best damn annual bonfire party at prestigious Waylon University, which is currently happening right now in the middle of a cotton field.

But…

I shouldn't even be at this party.

It's mostly for Greeks and jocks and popular people, yet here I am, a mere freshman, hanging out with my bubbly redheaded roommate, Skye.

"See?" she says as we take in the bonfire. "Isn't this better than watching cat videos on a Saturday night? What do you want to do first?"

I sigh, feeling nervous. Ever since I moved here from North Carolina, I've been pushing myself to try new things. Might as well put a crazy college party on that list. "Let's get a drink."

She claps and excitedly replies, "Done. Alcohol at two o'clock." We weave through the crowd, headed in that direction, and eventually we reach the bar, which is really just a long collapsible table someone set up. On top are various bottles of alcohol, and I grab the Fireball to pour shots. I've just tossed mine back and set down my cup when a prickling sensation washes over me, giving me goose bumps.

My gaze moves across the crowd, stopping on a tall guy with dark blond hair, broad shoulders, and a cocky smile. *Aha.* He's been staring at me, and now that he's caught, he raises his glass as a half-grin crosses his face.

I blush wildly as I adjust my black cat-eye glasses. I'm not used to such blatant male attention.

Skye—who's followed the trajectory of my gaze—spits out part of her drink. "Oh my God, do you know who that is?"

"Obviously I should," I say dryly.

Her mouth flops open. "You really need to get out more."

My eyes drift back to him but keep moving as if I'm not staring. "So who is Mr. Hottie McParty Pants?"

"If you don't know him, you don't deserve to know. But, he's H-O-T—like Chris Hemsworth hot. I dare you to flirt with him." She wiggles her eyebrows at me, knowing full well that for some reason, I can't resist a dare. Normally rather reserved, a dare gives me permission to be someone I'm not.

So does Fireball. I sling back another shot.

"I'll bring you a donut every day for a week if you flirt with him," she adds, watching me.

My ears perk up. "The ones with edible glitter?"

She nods, and I toss a quick glance back to him. Our eyes collide again, and a zing of connection fires between us. He has a strong, handsome face and a stance that has masculine written all over it. A smile tips up his full sensuous lips, and—

Two brunettes—twins, no less—approach him, one on either side, and wrap their arms around his waist. He smiles down at them. *Oh. Well then.*

I turn back to Skye and frown. "Player. Not interested."

She waves her hands in my face. "He likes you—I saw it on his face."

I snort. "Probably gas pains. Your dare is not accepted."

We hear our names being called from the other side of the party and turn to take in the helmet-haired Martha approaching us, which is taking some time due to the fact that she's wearing stilettos and a slinky halter dress. She carefully picks her way through the crowd, nudging people out of her way—sometimes rudely—as she focuses on us. *Great.*

"Incoming mean girl," I mutter under my breath.

Like us, Martha Burrows is a freshman and lives on our floor. Rather full of herself, she announced within a week of meeting us that she'd no longer answer to anything but *Muffin*, a nickname she'd given herself.

She eyes us both, a look of superiority on her pretty face. "I didn't know you two were invited to this little shindig. Obviously, I know all the right people, so I'm always invited." Her gaze zeroes in on my outfit and she rears back. "What on earth are you wearing, Nerd Girl?"

"Clothes." I stiffen at her name for me as I tug on my fitted Star Wars shirt and the pleated red miniskirt I made from a man's shirt. My long pale blonde hair is up in curled pigtails, and I went a bit heavy-handed with the shimmery eye shadow and red lipstick. It's not your typical look for WU—which is anything monogrammed—but I'm learning to ignore the raised eyebrows.

Skye, the peacemaker among us three, clears her throat and nods her head at the guy who's been staring. "Delaney has an admirer, but she doesn't know who he is."

Martha-Muffin follows Skye's gaze, eyeballing the mystery man over my shoulder. She gives me an exasperated look. "That's Maverick Monroe, you idiot. He's the biggest football star in Mississippi and the freshman recruit of the year. Word is, though, girls like you aren't his type—not at all." Her hand flicks a stiff honey-colored curl over her shoulder.

My teeth grind together. "Martha, if you think I care what you think about me and whether or not a quasi-famous football player is interested in me, then you are confused."

Her lips tighten. "It's *Muffin* now, and why do you have to use such big words? What does *quasi* even mean?" is her cutting reply.

Skye's eyes get as big as saucers, and I assume it's because Martha-Muffin and I are about to finally have it out. I can't stand her, and she can't stand me. We just…clash.

But that isn't what has Skye in such a titter.

She points over my shoulder, and I get it.

It's the person standing behind me, the one I can't see. I feel a nervous sneeze coming on and—*thank God*—I somehow push it down.

A husky voice reaches my ears. "*Quasi* means *seemingly* or *supposedly*. What she means is I'm probably not a famous football player but rather one that's been highly touted but is without merit."

Oh, shit. The voice is rich and smooth with just enough southern drawl to make a girl swoon. He also sounds halfway intelligent.

I turn around slowly. Mr. Tall, Blond, and Football is right in front of me wearing a cocky smile.

How in the hell did he get over here so fast?

You know that moment when everything stops and the next breath you take is the first one of the rest of your life? That's what it feels like as Maverick Monroe stares at me with his piercing blue eyes.

I glance down and take in the sculpted chest and hard biceps.

I look back up and see a chiseled jawline that's defined and lined with a slight scruff. I see the thin pink scar that slices through his left eyebrow, and it does nothing to detract from his appeal.

He's perfection.

He's air.

Which I desperately need right now, because I can't breathe.

He smirks, as if reading my mind, and I scramble to pull myself together. Someone calls his name—it's a girl's voice, probably one of those twins—but he doesn't budge.

His eyes rove over my skirt, glasses, and lips. "The question is…do you even know what makes a good football player?"

"Nice hands?"

His lips twitch. "Hardly."

"A tight end?" I smirk, feeling sassy…which is weird. I

don't know who I am right now, but it's like my mouth has a life of its own, saying things I normally wouldn't.

Martha-Muffin chokes on her drink at my remark and Skye watches me with glee, clearly excited that I have the attention of someone who is apparently *very* important at Waylon.

I put my hand on my hip. "The question is…why do I need to know?"

"You don't. All you need to know is I'm the best."

I suck in a little breath at his arrogance.

A guy walks past us and claps him on the shoulder. "Badass game last week, Mav. Rock on."

"Thanks, man." Maverick acknowledges the compliment and lifts his chin, his eyes never straying from mine.

"What position do you play?" I ask. "Quarterback?"

He smirks. "Middle linebacker—defense."

"Sounds fancy."

He laughs.

Skye, who's been eavesdropping unabashedly, sighs with a dreamy expression on her face. "His stats are the best in the country." She clears her throat. "I-I only know that because my brother is a huge fan, I swear."

"Hi, Maverick," Martha-Muffin says as she edges closer to him, nudging me out of the way with her sharp shoulders. "Remember me?"

He focuses on her. "No."

She glowers. "I was in your dorm room with your room-mate last week. You said *hello* to me."

He shrugs. "A lot of girls come through. I can't remember them all."

Oh. My. God. He *is* arrogant, but I like how he just shut her down.

Martha-Muffin's face reddens and she mutters something under her breath, flips around, and flounces off. Good riddance.

Out of the corner of my eye, I see Skye is drifting away too, giving me a thumbs-up.

Whatever. I am not going to flirt with this guy...am I?

He's definitely got something about him, something that makes my body buzz. I tilt my chin up, taking in how tall he is. He has to be at least six-four.

His gaze drifts over my face. "You know there's a legend here at Waylon about our famous bonfire party?"

"Oh?"

He smiles, a flash of white on his handsome face. "Legend says the first person you kiss at the party is the one you'll never forget. It might be years later, and still their face is the one you dream about."

"Sounds like hocus-pocus."

He lifts that mesmerizing left eyebrow. "I like to believe in legends—after all, I am one."

I smirk. "Probably a game made up by some frat-boy-slash-jock wanting to kiss all the girls."

He pauses for a moment as if thinking, and then he steps in closer, so close that I can see the varying shades of blue around his pupils. "May I?"

My heart does somersaults.

"May you what?" I ask, my voice low, but I know what he wants. My body is already leaning toward him, wanting it too.

"This." He kisses me, an almost imperceptible touch as he brushes his full lips against mine. The contact of our mouths is electric, sparks of fire skating along my skin.

As if from a distance, I hear someone calling his name. It's a female, and she's pissed.

It's one of the twins probably.

And I'm jealous.

But, I don't look. We pull away, and I stare at him as he stares right back. A stillness settles over the party, although I don't think anything's actually changed. The music is still playing. People are still talking. Beers are being passed around.

Yet...

We're connected.

Two stars in the black velvet sky.

Two ships passing in the night.

Oh, fuck, stop the nonsense, I tell myself.

"What was that?" I ask, my voice breathless.

"That's your first kiss of the bonfire. Now you'll never forget me."

And then, before I can think of a reply, he's gone.

I watch him go back to the twins, frustration coiling inside of me as I exhale.

It would be two years before I kissed him again.

CHAPTER 1

DELANEY

It's Valentine's Day evening, and my social life is worse than when I was a brace-faced freshman at William Henry Prep School in Charlotte, North Carolina. At least back then one of the geeks from my math class gave me a tiny heart-shaped box of stale chocolates and a brown teddy bear. All I have this year is a broken heart, a bottle of premium vodka, and an eighties horror movie.

Skye is out having fun, and I'm glad for her. She left the off-campus house we share earlier for a date with her boyfriend, Tyler, and here I sit…languishing in yoga pants and crying into my popcorn.

I send a longing glance at my phone, waiting for it to buzz with a call or text from someone who cares about me…but it remains silent, mocking me as I press myself into the worn brown leather of the sofa. I hate feeling sorry for myself, but sometimes it gets to me that I don't have any family since my Nana—the person who raised me—passed right before I left for college.

God. I'm lonely.

My nose takes a whiff of the blanket that's pulled up to my face, and I swear I still smell leftover hints of my ex's spicy cologne. Alex is a special teams kicker for the football team at Waylon, and we'd been together since we met in a literature class freshman year. He was my first, the person I thought I'd spend the rest of my life with, and for the past year, part of me half-expected him to propose. Instead, he cheated.

I take a sip of Grey Goose straight from the bottle, eyeing it balefully. At least he had great taste in vodka.

I lift the bottle in the air, toasting. "Happy Valentine's Day, Alex, wherever you are. I hope Martha-Muffin can give you what I couldn't—ideally, the clap."

Yep, my arch nemesis from freshman year slept with my boyfriend, and the worst part was I'd walked in on them in his dorm room.

Feeling that familiar melancholy of being alone creep in, I turn my attention back to the movie. Eerie, spooky music escalates from the surround sound speakers as a girl runs through a forest, her head twisting as she looks to see if she's being followed. Terror is stamped on her face.

It was on Skye's dare that I chose this particular flick, and part of me knows she really just wants me to be preoccupied on a night when I'm alone.

The popcorn is still warm from the microwave as I pop some in my mouth and chew rather furiously, watching as the heroine on the screen is suddenly accosted by a burly figure with a mask. I scream—even though I knew it was coming—sending fluffy white kernels flying. Han Solo, my cat, stands and hisses at me, his black and white fur sticking straight out.

I've upended him from his comfy position on the couch.

"Sorry, little man."

Screw the dare. I'll take her punishment, which would no doubt be inventive. The last time I lost, she made me stand on a table in the cafeteria and call out, "My milkshake brings all the boys to the yard."

I scramble for the remote and mute it, wondering if it counts if I watch without the sound on. I *am* watching it, just minus all the bloodcurdling screams and spine-tingling music.

"Give me *Sixteen Candles* or *The Goonies* any freaking day —those are the best of the eighties," I mutter under my breath as I stare down at Han. "You agree?"

His head cocks ever so slightly. He gets me. I know he does.

I exhale and sit back down, tucking my legs underneath me as I lean my head back against the couch.

Ping!

My phone goes off with a text and I straighten up to retrieve it from the table.

My brow furrows at the unknown number. Usually those are telemarketers or scammers…but it's a local prefix.

I read the text. **Hey, sexy. I'm glad I have a library card because I was checking you out today. Do you have a Band-Aid? Because I scraped my knee falling for you.**

Two things happen at once: I half-giggle and half-snort, causing a coughing fit I quickly recover from. I *was* in the library this morning before my upper level psychology class to work on a paper, but I didn't notice anyone staring at me. Must be my bestie pulling a prank on me with someone else's phone.

I quickly type a response. **Skye? What happened to your date with Tyler?**

It's entirely possible she's feeling sorry for me, has skipped out for a minute to check on me, and is using Tyler's phone. Any minute now she's going to ask if I'm still watching Michael Myers.

Another text comes in. **I'm not on a date and I don't know a Skye. Is she as hot as you?**

Stop messing around, I send. **I've had a tiny bit of vodka…okay, a lot.**

I'm a dude. Swear to baby Jesus.

My brow wrinkles. Is it possible this isn't Skye? But then who is it?

How did you get this number? I type out.

You put up a listing on the Help Wanted board in the student center a while back. I saw you and got the number. I saw you again today at the library so it must be a sign for us to get together. Wanna hook up, babe?

Babe?

Hook up?

What an assuming ass, I think as mortification shoots through me. No one has answered the listing I put up looking for a male partner to take a salsa class with me. Thankfully, the posting didn't have my name on it (*so embarrassing*), just my phone number, and I've been meaning to take it down, but between working at the library and class, I haven't found the time. I was in a weak place when the idea struck, and now, looking back, it reeks of desperation from a girl who'd recently been cheated on and was lonely.

I glare at the phone as if the jerkwad on the other side can actually see me.

I'm not your personal Tinder, I reply, my fingers flying across the screen. **Go find someone else to harass.**

Nothing comes through for the next fifteen minutes as I stare blindly at the television, not really seeing anything, just fuming, my mind racing through possibilities of who saw me posting the ad. Hundreds of students pass through every day, and it could have been anyone. I think back to my morning study session today at the library, trying to recall if anyone was watching me, but I was hyper-focused (as usual) and kept my head down.

I should probably block this number.

A new text pings.

Hey, look, I'm sorry. This isn't the person with the horrible pick-up lines and offer of sex who first texted you. Those messages were from my asshole friend who took my phone and texted you without my knowledge. I have it back now so we're cool, right? Sorry for the inconvenience and I hope you find a salsa partner. Later.

Finally, a polite text—except for the goodbye part, because I wasn't done talking. I still want to know who these two people are. Part of me wonders if it's Alex, feeling me out, maybe seeing if I've moved on. He has been texting me, trying to engage me in a dialogue, but I've ignored him. This doesn't seem like his style though.

Hold your horses, stalker. Who are you?

Seconds tick by and I can see the dots on the screen indicating he's replying. I'm picturing a loser at a frat house, the first one to fall asleep, and instead of drawing a giant dick on his forehead, they stole his phone and texted random girls.

My name is Inigo Montoya. You killed my father. Prepare to die.

I laugh under my breath at the iconic movie reference and part of me relaxes. **Good one,** I text.

You're a fan of *The Princess Bride*?

One of my favorites. I even have a t-shirt with Buttercup and Westley on it, I type, referring to the two main characters.

I'll remember that.

Is that why you're texting me on Valentine's Day? To talk about *The Princess Bride*? **Are you lonely?** My fingers move quickly, feeling comforted that I'm not the only one who's a romance dud on the holiday of love.

I'm texting you because my friend was a jerk. He doesn't mean to be; he just thinks we should hook up.

Not going to touch that comment.

So where are you right now? Dorm? Frat party? Off-campus strip club? My detective cap is on and I'm determined to figure out who this guy is. My mind goes back to a rather geeky, thin guy who hangs out in the romance section at the library. He's given me a few lingering glances when I happen to walk past him.

I'm in bed, he says.

Alone? I'm being bolder than usual.

Yes. You?

I'm hesitant about responding. After all, he could be a serial killer, but I don't get that vibe, and I trust my instincts.

Just me and my cat, a scary movie, and a bottle of vodka—hell of a way to spend V-Day.

At least two minutes go by—a damn long time in the world of texting—and I wonder if he's left or grown bored of me. Chewing on my bottom lip, I'm in the middle of chastising myself for revealing as much as I have when a new message comes in.

Is it crazy and weird that we're talking and you don't know who I am?

Do you know who I am? I ask, adjusting my cat-eye glasses on my nose. If he saw me put up the ad, he probably does. Waylon is small, with an enrollment of around six thousand, so it's likely we've seen each other or even had a class together.

You're Delaney, a junior from North Carolina.

My pulse kicks up as I feel my heart beating in my chest, but those are basic facts he could have gotten off my social media.

He sends another text. **Truth: I think you're gorgeous. We also know each other…sorta.**

He thinks I'm gorgeous? My bruised ego is flattered, and I shoot a look at Han. "Did it just get a little hot in here or is that the vodka talking?" He rolls his eyes and flounces off to the kitchen. "Are you saying I've had too much?" I call after him, but he pointedly ignores me by not turning around.

I stare down at my phone, wondering what else to say. I should probably end this, but I feel an odd connection with my new texting partner.

I could talk to a random guy.

I want to.

Do it, Delaney. I mentally dare myself.

Are you still there? he says. **Did I go too far? I tend to do that. I should just apologize in advance for anything I'm about to say or do.**

He hasn't gone too far. My interest is piqued. **So who are you?**

I'm a badass athlete.

I roll my eyes. **So you play a sport here at Waylon?**

Yes.

Crap. My heart does a little sputter and takes a nosedive— it's likely he knows Alex. The athletic dorm is situated on the west side of campus, and most of the players reside there. Football, baseball, and wrestling take up one side of Byrd Hall, while soccer, volleyball, tennis, and the minor sports occupy the other.

I purse my lips. **Which sport? I've sworn off football for the moment.**

Let's keep that a secret, but if you need a name, you can call me He-Man.

And I'll be She-Ra?

His reply is swift. **Hell no—they were siblings. Pick another name, something that suits you.**

Does He-Man suit you? I type. **Do you live at Castle Grayskull? Are you fighting Skeletor?**

Damn straight. I kick his ass every day.

I grin. **You're very serious about this. I'm starting to wonder if you might be crazy.**

Just pick.

Princess Leia.

Perfect, he replies. **I'm picturing you with cinnamon buns on your head.**

I giggle. **I'm picturing you as a muscled blond dude with a brain the size of a walnut.**

Don't be fooled by the dumb jock stereotypes.

And you shouldn't be fooled by my nerdy, quiet girl status. I'm a red-blooded woman with needs. *God.* I can't believe I just typed that. I take another sip of vodka. **What I MEANT to say is I don't do athletes anymore, specifically football players.** *Okay, that sounded stupid.* Clearly, I need to stop texting.

Nothing comes back from him, and my mind wanders.

Is he a football player? That might explain why he's not telling me his name. The guys on the team have a serious bro code when it comes to not messing with the exes of the other players.

I decide to change the subject. **My roommate dared me to watch a scary movie tonight—alone. I was terrified.**

Do you like dares? he texts.

Yes. It forces me to put myself out there. It feels silly to say, but it's easy to tell him because I don't *know* him. I'm beginning to see why anonymity is attractive.

I hear Han meowing at the back door. He has a litter box in the laundry room, but he's rather manly and likes to go out for an occasional romp around the yard to mark his territory. I like to go with him since my last cat disappeared on me a year ago, leaving me devastated.

Hey, I need to go, I tell my mystery man. **My cat needs me.**

Wait, you said you take dares, right?

Yes.

I dare you to dream about me tonight.

What? Why? I ask, my heart rate picking up a beat.

Because I'll dream about you.

Oh. I bite my lip and chew on it. **Like a sexy dream?**

Is that what you want?

Yes.

My body comes alive, every sense on alert. It feels like forever since someone kissed me or made my stomach feel fluttery inside.

I type out, **I need more details if I want to picture you in my head, especially since I don't know who you are.**

You know I'm an athlete, I'm blond, and I like to swing my sword around.

I giggle. **Where are we in the dream? Give me a setting. I need more.**

A few moments go by before he finally responds. **At a frat party. Everyone else is downstairs and you and I are upstairs in an empty bathroom.**

Seriously?

This is my fantasy, Princess Leia. Just listen.

Fine. What are we doing? The room feels warmer, and my fingers are sweaty as I type the words. I picture myself with a dark shadowy male in a tiny cramped bathroom. His hands cup my face as he stares down at me, his thumb tracing over my lips. He kisses me on the neck, sending lightning bolts of sensation across my skin.

My body heats to the point that I squirm around on the

couch, fingers hovering over my phone.

What do you think we're doing? he texts.

Kissing?

More.

Shit. **Second base?**

More.

Home run? I send after a slight pause, feeling lightheaded. This has escalated and I'll probably regret it tomorrow, but for right now, I don't care.

We're going at it against the wall, Princess Leia—hard. I like it hard.

I picture it, the small bathroom hot with our proximity. My body arches toward his and he barely has his jeans shoved down yet he's inside me, sliding in and out as I moan…

Shit. This has gotten totally out of control. The feisty girl-power woman in me is rebelling at the suggestion of him taking me hard, but…*holy smokes*, I like it. My heart thunders.

Are you still there?

I type, **I have to go.**

As you wish.

With a flurry of motion, I turn my phone off and toss it down on the couch. He-Man or Badass Athlete or whatever he calls himself is trouble. I stare at my phone for a few more beats before dashing to the kitchen to drink down a glass of ice-cold water.

CHAPTER 2

DELANEY

I am crazy late for class as I jog out of the student center coffee shop. Wearing my black fitted North Face jacket and carrying my huge backpack, I'm a bit unsteady on my feet. I clutch a large coffee in one hand and a donut in the other; both are essential, sweet sustenance and the best part of my morning, especially since I have to head to the farthest corner of campus for my class.

My head is bent down as I head out the glass doors, my gaze catching on a silver Porsche as it screeches to a halt in a primo parking spot near the entrance.

Ugh. It's Alex, and I do not want to see him.

My fists clench as I take a step back under the shadow of the portico, hoping I can skirt over to the right to miss him before he sees me. Even though he's constantly sending texts asking to meet up, I'm not ready. He's even shown up at my door a few times, but I either don't answer or I have Skye tell him I'm not there.

I'm the unluckiest person alive because before I can turn away, his brown eyes find my face. He pauses, his cheeks reddening. Maybe it's from the cold that's still hovering this Monday morning, or perhaps he's embarrassed. He freaking should be. I recall how he gave me a promise ring on our one-year anniversary, saying he couldn't wait to make it a real engagement ring. Obviously, his "promise" meant nothing.

He throws a tentative hand up as if he wants to wave, but then it falls flat and rests against his leg.

Dammit. I can't deal with this confrontation right now. Catching him in the act nearly broke me.

I flip around and barge down the path to get away from him.

His voice follows me, echoes of a timbre that used to send shivers down my spine. "Hey, Delaney! Wait up."

No. No matter how much I want to go off on him, I'm not stopping. My Converse eat up the sidewalk as I keep my head down and stare at my shoelaces. *Just keep going, just keep going—*

Smack.

I run straight into another body, one that smells faintly of something I can't put my finger on, something…exotic and dark.

All I catch in that brief moment is that he's tall, maybe six-four, with a chest of steel. My coffee sails through the air and lands upside down in the landscaping that lines the walk. I curse. I hadn't even taken a good long sip yet because it was too hot.

Then, just when I think I've managed to keep my donut safe, my feet get tangled and I stumble again into the blond Viking, pressing my donut into his broad chest.

"Dammit," is the gruff word that comes out of him as his hands reach out to my shoulders. His touch is firm and steadying without overpowering me, as if he's completely aware of his strength and I'm merely a wisp in his grasp—well, maybe not a wisp. I'm five-ten, and I can hold my own around a big guy.

"Could you watch where you're going, please?" he says, a flare of annoyance in his tone.

"You're the one who plowed into me," I snap back. This is not true, but I'm angry.

I lift my head and meet piercing blue eyes that make me go hot all over. Clear and warm, they have a hint of gray around the iris, giving them a steely look. He blinks as he takes me in, raking his eyes over my messy bun, bulky coat, and leggings. I am not dressed to impress, my face bare of makeup save for quick swipes of lip gloss and mascara, my eyebrows in serious need of waxing. I tuck a strand of pale blonde hair that has fallen out of my bun behind my ear, groaning inwardly. Leave it to me to not only see my ex but run into the unattainable and enigmatic Maverick Monroe immediately after.

My first memory of him is freshman year at the fall bonfire party. He showed up with twins, one on each arm, but somehow he ended up kissing *me*, claiming some legend about the person you kiss at your first bonfire at Waylon being the one person you never forget.

Yeah right.

He had forgotten about me—obviously—and I'd moved on and met Alex, who at the time was sweet and kind, not the cheating asshole he is now.

In the background, I hear Alex's voice from behind me, calling my name, but the warrior in front of me has all my attention. Maverick is the one football player our team couldn't live without. All hard muscle and strength, our defense is legendary in the Southeastern Conference, and it's largely because of him, the hottest jock ever who thinks he's the best thing since hairless cats. Maybe he is. I wouldn't know because I don't really know him. Sure, I know he has washboard abs and shoulders that make you bite your lip, but I don't know a thing about his personal life.

I'm not his type.

Sadly, he *is* my type, right down to his tight jeans, Converse, and tight black shirt that accentuates every indentation in his chest. Why isn't he wearing a coat in February? Probably too tough.

"You okay?" he asks, his gaze drifting over me.

I clear my throat. "Yeah."

"I suppose you're on your way to class." He checks his watch. "Which starts in five minutes. Looks like we're both going to be late. At least you didn't get any coffee on you." He smiles, a flash of white teeth peeking through full, pouty lips.

I tell my eyes to stop looking at him—because football guys can't be trusted, *dammit*—but there are three things my brain can't help but notice: Mexican food, Star Wars, and a tightly muscled athlete…and donuts. So, four.

I nod. "Yeah, you sit with your fan girls in the middle of the auditorium. I sit in the back." I sigh as he plucks the donut off his chest. "Sorry for bumping into you. I was in a hurry to get there, I guess."

"No worries. It gives us a chance to talk."

What? *Why does he want to talk to me?*

"About what?" I ask, but he doesn't answer me.

Instead, he stares down at the pink and purple sprinkles and edible glitter that dot his shirt. "That's a lot of sugar on my shirt. That can't be good for you."

"I...sorry. The sprinkles are a weakness, and I can't resist getting them. I always say I'm not going to because they have to be at least another fifty calories, but in the end, they're just so pretty." I point to the squashed donut. "That particular one is called the Unicorn because it has every kind of sprinkle in the entire bakery on it." I make the sign of the cross. "Rest in peace, sweet donut."

I continue babbling about the different flavors of donuts as I hurriedly wipe at his shirt with my hands, flinging bits of dough to the sidewalk while secretly calculating if I have enough time to dash back in to grab another one.

His chest is—unsurprisingly—hard as iron, his pecs solid as my fingers fuss over him, and suddenly I'm feeling shy and self-conscious because I've touched him without permission. Sure, we briefly touched lips two years ago, but that seems like a lifetime ago.

I drop my hands to my sides and our eyes collide again.

A nervous sneeze threatens to erupt, and I push it down, my fingers clenching the straps of my backpack. *Don't do it, Delaney!*

He clears his throat. "I was wondering if you wanted—"

Alex appears next to me. "Delaney! Are you deaf? I've been calling your name and you didn't even turn around." His eyes bounce from me to Maverick, taking in the donut, which is still in Maverick's hand, along with my forlorn coffee cup sitting prettily atop an ornamental bush. "What happened?" he questions, his square face concerned, his eyes taking in my face slowly, lingering on my lips. He's a handsome guy, lean and wiry, with soft eyes, auburn hair, and an easy smile that used to make me melt.

My entire body tightens. We haven't spoken in a month, and now here he is, chasing me down across campus and looking at me like I'm a piece of candy.

"Aren't you even going to talk to me?" Alex hitches up his backpack and takes another step toward me.

Maverick turns his gaze to me and throws up an eyebrow, as if prompting me to respond. *He's rather desperate*, his expression seems to say.

I'd rather eat snails than talk to him, I say back with my face. I'm not sure he gets my body language message, but I could have sworn his lips twitched.

Either way, he says nothing, just slides his gaze from me to Alex.

I'm a bundle of nerves, and most of it has to do with Alex chasing after me, but some of it is because bumping into Maverick has me thinking back to Badass Athlete and what *he's* doing right now. What if Maverick *is* Badass Athlete? They're both blond and athletic…but what if Badass Athlete is just a tennis player? Or one of those volleyball dudes? There's a ton of them.

Alex takes my hand, and because I'm so surprised that he's touching me, I let him. "Look, babe, I don't want to have this conversation in front of everyone"—he sends some side-eye toward Maverick, who hasn't moved an inch—"but do you want to meet me at Pluto's for coffee after your class? I know you love that place."

Babe? Ugh.

"You asked what happened—we bumped into each other," Maverick says rather abruptly as his eyes go from me to Alex, talking as if everything is perfectly normal. He's trying to change the topic, and I appreciate it. Maybe he reads the desperation on my face. "Actually, I was on my phone—an emergency with my sister, but everything's okay. I was looking down, and I guess Delaney was too." He shrugs. "Unfortunately, she lost her breakfast in the process, and I lost my phone."

"Did you drop it?" I ask, checking him out and not seeing one in his hands.

He nods, and it's the perfect reason to immediately retract my hand from Alex's and bend down to see if I can find it. Maverick does the same, and our shoulders bump together as we pillage through the azaleas.

"Thank you," I whisper to him as we scan the sidewalk.

"For what?" he whispers back.

"For defusing that…moment."

"Ah—you're still into him."

I scowl. "No, I'm not."

"Then why are you so flustered?"

"I'm not," I huff out under my breath. Scrambling around in the bushes is not the place to explain the dynamics of my relationship with Alex.

"You are. Is it because you bumped into me?" A small grin

curls his lips, and I'm reminded of the arrogant football player I met at the bonfire.

I give him a glare. "No. I barely know you."

"We can change that." He cocks an eyebrow.

Oh.

Well then.

"I'm not one of your groupies. I don't do random hook-ups."

"Maybe I'm just trying to get to know you."

I give him a *get real* look. "Why? We barely talk."

His gaze flicks back to Alex, who's also looking for the phone a few feet away. "Now that you're not dating Alex…"

I let out a triumphant shout when I find the phone and hold it up over my head. Alex is glowering at us, and I think he has been since I pulled my hand out of his. I ignore him.

"Found it, and thankfully it didn't get wet from my coffee." Maverick and I stand together and do a little handoff where he gives me the crushed donut and I give him his phone. Our fingers graze, giving me a shiver of heat. I stick my hand in my coat pocket.

Alex touches my arm and shoots an annoyed look between Maverick and me. He's holding my empty coffee cup, retrieved from the shrubbery, and he also grabbed my small desk calendar, which slipped out of my backpack because I left it half-unzipped in my rush to get out of the house this morning.

"Here, don't you need this?" He waves it at me.

I give him a tight nod and shove it into my bag without looking at him.

"Are you okay? No bumps or bruises?" Alex asks, running

his hands over my shoulders.

"No, I'm fine." I straighten up and give my chin a little hitch to look at him. He's not as tall as Maverick, about six-one.

A built-up sigh I hadn't known I'd been holding in comes out, long and full of pent-up emotion. So what if Maverick is here, listening? It's not like the entire campus doesn't already know why we broke up. Gossip spreads like wildfire.

"What do you want, Alex? I have a class to get to."

He stiffens as he glances briefly at Maverick, who is curiously *still* standing here. "I just wanted to see you, and…say hello. Now that football is over, I thought we could get together and talk about everything. I never had the chance to tell you I'm sorry in person for…everything."

An image of him and Martha-Muffin in his bed flashes in my head. "You mean for cheating on me." *Get it right, asshole.*

Alex closes his eyes briefly then takes my elbow and gently pulls me aside.

With a sigh, I let him. Maybe if he can say what he needs to, he'll stop bothering me.

"Don't be like this, Delaney," he says in a lowered tone. "Muffin was a one-time thing. I swear I've never cheated on you before."

My heart aches at the memory. I shake my head. "You… you are not the person I thought you were. We're over, Alex."

He bites his lip, a pleading look in his eyes. "I just want things to go back to the way they were."

I take a deep breath, the urge to flee intense. "I have to get to class now."

I turn back around, and Maverick is still standing over near the hedge, his face concerned as he watches us. He calls my name as I stomp past, but I keep going.

I just need away from both of them. Football guys can suck it.

I imagine both of their eyes on me and barely resist throwing up a one-finger salute, but those cocky athletes aren't worth the energy it would take.

CHAPTER 3

DELANEY

Being an introvert comes with tells. Sometimes I giggle uncontrollably, but more often than not, I sneeze when I'm nervous. When I'm faced with a situation that tilts my world on its axis, a tingling starts up in my nose, itching and building pressure until finally I sneeze. Senior year of high school, I got caught skipping school, and when the principal called me into his office, I sneezed so many times tears poured down my face. He let me go after stuffing a box of Kleenex into my hands. Sometimes it works in my favor and I can use it as an excuse to make a quick exit, but sometimes it can just be downright annoying.

Like now.

"May I sit here?" a deep voice says from behind me.

My body knows who it is before my brain does, and right away, I suppress the pre-sneeze sensation by inhaling sharply and holding my breath for five seconds.

I slip my glasses down a few notches as I look over to see Maverick staring at me. It's been a couple of days since the donut tragedy, and we've passed each other in the hallway a few times. Once I thought he said something, but I'm too awkward to stop and say, *Hey, did you just say something to me?* so I just ignored him.

We're inside the auditorium for our psych class, and my hands flutter around the desk next to me. "Do whatever you want. Be prepared, though—the lights are rather dim back here. Wouldn't want you to fall asleep."

Somehow he manages to settle his large frame into the cushioned seat and reclines it back, him and his long jean-clad legs taking up all the space next to me—and the air.

"Ah, I could never fall asleep here." He shoots me a grin, and I mentally put up my shields. *Don't get sucked into the hotness.*

I nod, making small talk. "Yeah, it's an interesting class."

"And you're in it."

My lashes flutter and I can't bring myself to look at him. I just can't. A normal person would ask what he meant by that, but this is me. I just clear my throat and scoot my leg over a little to give him more room.

Just be cool, Delaney.

"What are you drawing?" he asks, leaning over my shoulder.

I stop the doodling I've been doing in my notebook. The heat from his body is intoxicating, and I swallow. "Han Solo."

His lips twitch. "Hate to break it to you, Buttercup, but Han Solo isn't a cat. He's the captain of the Millennium Falcon."

"He's also a scoundrel and a smuggler," I add. "And who gave you permission to call me Buttercup?"

He waves that off and says, "I know he's a scoundrel—it's

what makes him endearing. He's a badass and also has the best friend ever, a seven-foot-tall Wookie with a gun. He's my favorite Star Wars character ever, next to Yoda."

Maverick likes Star Wars? I just assumed he sat around and watched recordings of football games while guzzling beer with a girl on either side of him.

I nod and point to my doodle. "Named my cat after him, Han Solo #2."

"What happened to #1? Killed by a light saber?"

I laugh. "I hope she ran off with a tomcat. She's probably living in a tree house with her baby kittens right now." I don't tell him I cried for a month when she disappeared. I don't actually know what happened to her, but imagining her with a sweet little family is the vision I like to keep close to my heart.

"Living the dream," he says, and I flick my eyes at him. He's hard to look at full-on, but I do, letting our eyes meet, my green and his pale blue. Almost iridescent, like a glittering opal, they contrast vividly with his tanned skin. His chin is firm and square with the hint of a cleft in the middle, and his hair is a mixture of dark blond with streaks of gold, painted by the sun from all those days of practicing football. I can't see his scar from this angle but I know it's there, on the other side of his face, that one little imperfection.

A slight smile curves his lips as his eyes warm, and I seize up, realizing I've been staring about ten seconds too long. That kind of stare means you either want to kill someone or sleep with them, and I've just crossed that line.

"Delaney?"

He says my name softly, and my mouth dries up as a shot

of electricity shoots straight to my core.

Good grief, ignore this weird hormonal reaction you have to Maverick.

Right. Now.

"You okay?" he asks.

He thinks I'm an idiot.

"Fine, totally fine. How's it going? How's football? Oh, yeah, it's over…but you're still practicing, right? To get ready for next year and all? Can't believe we'll be seniors. Also can't believe you decided to stay another year when you could have been drafted." I'm rambling and my voice sounds breathy. I gulp in a deep inhalation to steady myself.

He scratches his head, a bemused expression on his face. "You're funny."

"I don't talk much, but when I do, I make the most of it."

He laughs. "I stayed because I wouldn't have been picked early enough yet. I need to build my stats if I want the best deal. I have a buddy who went early and his contract sucked. I have another friend who waited it out and got a two million dollar deal."

"It's all about the money."

"Especially if you've never had it," he adds.

Interesting. Maybe Maverick didn't grow up with much. I think back to what I know about him, and I realize it's basically nothing, except that he's from Magnolia. I stare down at my doodle. I'm not rich like Alex, but I do okay with the money Nana left me. I own the house Skye and I live in, and I don't have to work a full-time job. Thankfully, I'm at WU on an art scholarship.

I glance back up at him. "So…why is the big guy on campus sitting in the back of the auditorium with me? Isn't there a football groupie somewhere crying because you aren't next to her?"

"Because I can." He pauses. "And you aren't dating Alex anymore."

"What does that mean?" I can't believe I asked, but something about him has me feeling reckless.

He gets a tight look on his face. "Just an observation. You've been with him since freshman year, and everyone thought you guys were the perfect couple."

"I didn't think you cared—you know, with the twins and all."

"You remember the bonfire." It's not a question.

"Kinda hard to forget."

His eyes find mine. "I gave you your first kiss at the bonfire. Legend says you'll never forget me."

I tilt my head. "What's your name again?"

He laughs, but soon a cloud seems to settle on the planes of his chiseled face. "Alex isn't over you."

"Why do you say that?"

His shoulders shift, the movement barely perceptible yet giving off a visceral impression of suppressed power.

"He's my teammate, and I see how he looks at you. He wasn't happy to see us standing together on Monday, and that was just an accidental run-in. Imagine how he'd react if there really *was* something between us." His eyes slide over to my face. "He'd probably freak out and get pissed at me, and it would definitely screw up his game, and then *poof*, there goes our chance at a championship next year." He gives me a teasing look. "Kickers are rather emotional…"

I wrinkle my nose. "Regardless if any of that's true or not, I do what I want."

He studies me intently. "So you're dating again?"

"Why do you care anyway?" I ask.

"Hey, Mav, aren't you going to come sit with us?" It's a sleek-looking girl with dark hair and a lot of hot pink lipstick speaking from behind the railing that lines the back of the auditorium. Miss Brunette trails her finger along his shoulder, giving him a soft caress.

She sends a half-smile my way, clearly not worried about me being any kind of competition. I don't reciprocate.

He flicks his gaze at her, showing even white teeth as he smiles at her, but it doesn't ring true. They chat about class, and I'm fascinated, watching his reaction to everything she says, taking in the way he nods, the non-interest in his gaze. His eyes find mine as she rambles on and on about some big off-campus mixer between the frat houses, and he smiles ever so slightly.

He isn't into her, and I know it.

I don't know how I'm able to read him, but it's as if we have a connection and I *get* him.

She walks off, hips swaying as she does another little wave over her shoulder.

"You sleep with her?" I ask casually.

He shrugs. "A few times last year."

Ah. "You're just a playboy, aren't you?"

"I've had relationships."

I narrow my eyes at him, feeling prickly. "Yeah? What's the longest one?"

He cocks a smile. "Dated a sweet girl back in high school for a year…" His voice trails off. "Then things got messed up and I came to Waylon. Football's been my muse ever since."

"Doesn't that get, I don't know, lonely?"

He stares at me. "Is this an interview?"

"No. I don't even care." Total lie. I'm dying to know the scoop on Maverick.

A gruff laugh comes out of him. "I just know when a girl's a keeper and when she isn't. She wasn't."

"Ah, a keeper—I see."

"Yeah, you know, the one girl who makes your heart pound like crazy every time she walks into the room." He's looking at me with an intensity that makes me breathless.

Does he mean me?

Don't be ridiculous.

Just then the professor enters and begins his lecture, so I pull out my iPad to bring up the class website and get to work.

I try really hard to ignore how close Maverick is sitting, how his leg occasionally brushes against mine…and I remind myself that getting interested in a cocky-as-hell football player is the last thing I need right now.

CHAPTER 4

MAVERICK

It's the same dream again. I try to pull myself out of it, but it's no use.

Maybe the outcome will be different this time.

Rain slaps at the car and Def Leppard blares on the radio as my father drives our old van. My mother yells at him, her mouth moving in slow motion, the sound disembodied, as if my brain doesn't want to hear her words. I look over at my little sister and curl my hand into hers. She's scared, and I have to protect her.

Dread snakes down my spine when a diesel truck's horn blares at us as we fly past it, our headlights reflecting off his grill.

It's coming.

My body tenses…waiting.

Just around this hairpin curve.

I have to stop him.

I yell at Dad to slow down.

I scream at Mom to shut up.

But I never say it in time.

There's a deer in the road, its brown face turning to look straight into our headlights.

There's a horrible metallic sound, like tin foil wrapping around a piece of meat, and then stifling silence, thick with smoke and fumes. Gas...I smell gas and oil, and it makes me frantic. I'm just seventeen, but I've seen movies—I know cars blow up. *Maybe it would be better if it did*, I think to myself in my dream. If we all just died, everything would be okay.

No, I tell myself. *Get out. Live.*

I touch my skin, feeling glass. Blood covers my fingers. Dangling from the seat belt, somehow I fight to break free and manage to crawl out of the mangled heap. Mom lies on the pavement, her body twisted like a pretzel.

I hear a whimper and find Raven, a broken doll, her eyes shut as I turn her over—

God, make it stop. Fuck!

I jerk myself awake, my body in a full sweat. Rubbing my hands through my hair, I glance at the clock and exhale heavily. It's five o'clock in the morning, and there's no way in hell I can go back to sleep after that nightmare.

My bedroom door opens, and it's Ryker, one of my roommates and my best friend. We live in an apartment-style suite in Byrd Hall, also known as the athletic dorm. He squints at me with bleary red eyes. "Dude? Heard you thrashing around—you all right?"

I scrub my face one final time and get out of bed, willing my heart rate to slow down. "Same old shit."

"Car wreck?" He leans on the doorjamb and gives me a concerned once-over. He's our quarterback, a big dude with a heart of gold, and he knows the fucked-up childhood I lived through.

I nod quickly. "Every time February rolls around, it brings it all back. It's like I'm in the dream and I keep thinking I can stop it from happening, but I never do."

He nods, studying my face. "It doesn't help that you're worried about Raven. Your dad needs to get his shit straight."

A muscle ticks in my jaw. Just thinking about him makes my blood boil. He's lost his latest job as a mechanic...again.

"How's she doing?" he asks me.

"As best she can."

A sigh comes from him, and I know he's got an opinion. "You're wearing yourself out going to see her every afternoon. Hell, it was midnight before you got in last night. Between practice and her...something's got to give."

My mouth compresses. "I don't have a choice."

Raven suffered a traumatic brain injury, also known as a TBI, in the accident. Now, at nineteen, she drags her right leg and has speech issues, and don't even get me started on the loss of cognitive ability and emotional outbursts. Worry tugs at me as I think about everything she's lost.

Everything I lost.

She's been staying with my dad temporarily for the past few weeks since we removed her from the state-funded group home where she'd lived since the car wreck three years ago.

I never liked the home with its tiny rooms and smell of death, and when she showed up with unexplained bruises on her skin a few weeks ago, I knew right away that I had to get her out of there. I removed her and placed her with my dad, but she needs *somewhere* besides his trailer. She needs stability and a routine and a regular nursing staff to check on her every single day, not just the one her disability helps pay for that only comes out three days a week.

If only I had known about the abuse before I'd signed the paperwork to not go into the draft early. I let out a deep breath. Now it's too late, and I have to wait until next year.

"You should talk to Coach Al—maybe he can help." He's saying what he always does, but Ryker doesn't get it. No one does.

"Help with what?" I can't help but be annoyed with him. "Going out to my dad's trailer and cooking dinner? Helping her get in the shower? Getting her ready for bed? Get real, man. I need *money*, and no one affiliated with football or Waylon can do that because it would be an infraction with the NCAA. I can't accept any compensation or donations, remember? Coach can't even buy me a fucking candy bar. If they think any kind of money or benefits changed hands—for anything—I'll be out of a career in the NFL. Those are the goddamn rules."

"Stupid rules," he mutters. "If you weren't such a damn fine player…"

Yeah, tell me about it.

"I'm cool, okay. Things will work out," I say with a lightness I'm not feeling, playing off my worry. I show him my fists, which are rough and red from hitting the punching bag at Carson's Gym, an off-campus facility I've been sparring at for extra cardio. "I work out my frustrations this way."

He shakes his head. "You always get all squirrely on me this time of year. Do me a favor and get laid, or ask that girl out."

"What girl?"

He sends me an *are you kidding me?* look. "Dude, don't even pretend."

I ignore him, grab my socks out of the drawer, and slide them on while he watches me like a mother hen.

"And we need to talk about this fight thing, man. I'm worried." His voice has lowered and he's whispering, and I assume he doesn't want the chick in his bedroom to hear.

I pause. I confessed to him last week that a casino owner, Leslie Brock, was at the gym where I spar and offered me a flat fee if I would box another college football player at his casino. No one would ever know, and it would be enough money to get Raven set up somewhere.

"If anyone finds out, *that* will ruin your fucking career. Look at Michael Vick—went to jail just for financing a dog fighting ring."

I groan. We've had this conversation. "No one's getting arrested, and Vick was running a million-dollar operation with illegal gambling, plus he killed the dogs that refused to fight. I'm not gambling or killing animals for sport. I'd just be fighting for money."

That said, it is risky as hell, and I haven't decided if I'm going through with it.

His lips flatten. "You really don't know what this guy is planning. Who the hell knows if it's even legal? I can see it now: you'll be wearing an orange jumpsuit *and* taking it up the ass."

I snort. "Someone else would be my bitch."

He huffs, letting out a sigh of frustration. "He owns a casino, and that shit will blow up the NCAA rules."

I stop getting dressed and give him a long look. We've been friends since freshman year when we met on the field, so by now I've known him long enough to see that he needs reassuring, just like he does when I slap him on the back and tell him his arm is fucking golden and he's going to take us to a championship next year.

He might be the quarterback, but I'm the glue that holds our defense together, the glue he needs.

I push out a grin even though I don't feel like it. "Dude, I'm not getting arrested. Next year is going to be our year for a championship, and there's no fucking way I'd jeopardize that."

Except when it comes to my sister.

He nods, the scowl lifting, revealing his All-American face that is usually lit up with a permanent grin. "I knew you'd make the right decision. You know if you ever need any money, I can maybe see if one of my relatives has some extra cash. It's a long shot, but—"

My pride jacks its head up. I was the recipient of a lot of handouts growing up, and I never want to revisit that. "No, I'm cool. I'm making it."

"Ryker, where'd you go?" comes the sleepy voice of the jersey chaser in his bed.

I arch my brow at him, recognizing the nasally whine even with a wall between us. "Is that Muffin? Seriously? Don't tell her shit. Her mouth is bigger than your ass." I pause. "I thought she was doing Alex now?"

I've never been with her, but half the team has. A bit of a schemer, she's never gotten over the fact that I turned her down cold freshman year when she snuck into my room one night and tried to crawl in bed with me.

Ryker shakes his head. "Apparently that was a one-time thing. Alex is probably still in love with you know who." He cocks an eyebrow and I know he's waiting for me to comment about Delaney, but I don't—not going there. Yeah, I'm interested in her, always have been, but she *is* my teammate's ex, and that's touchy.

"*Rykeeerrrrr*, I need you, big man," she coos from the other room, her voice making a weird throaty sound.

I suppress a laugh. "Sounds like you're being paged, bro, and FYI, she's looking for a paycheck, so instead of worrying about me fighting, maybe worry about Muffin pulling a fast one on you. Wrap it when you tap it."

"You're just trying to change the subject," he mumbles.

I've finished dressing so I grab my shoes and shove them on. Once I'm ready, I put on my orange and blue Waylon Wildcats cap and jog past him into the small living area we share with two other players. A quick glance tells me their doors are still shut and I haven't woken them up. *Good.*

He follows me and stands there glaring, concern on his face. "Where you going?"

"For a run." I chug down a bottle of Gatorade from the fridge in the kitchenette.

"At five in the morning? It's still dark—you might get run over." He's got an obstinate look on his face.

"I'll stick to the sidewalks and areas with streetlights."

"At least wear pants. It's cold as shit out there."

I huff out a laugh. "Dude, are you sure you aren't a girl?"

He shrugs. "Just worry about you is all."

"Bye, Mom," I say sarcastically as I head out the door.

CHAPTER 5

DELANEY

He-Man: Are you over your ex?

Me: Why?

He-Man: Just curious. Do you miss him?

Me: Sometimes. But every day is better.

He-Man: You just have to get your groove back. I dare you to go to the library and shout out that Princess Leia is a badass.

Me: What? No!

He-Man: I thought you couldn't turn down a dare.

Me: How will you know if I go through with it?

He-Man: Oh, I'll be there watching. What time should I show up?

Me: Dammit. Tomorrow at 8:00 PM. BTW, I hate you.

☺

I smile, feeling good as I think about today's text convo with He-Man. We've been texting on and off for the past week, just little messages here and there. He now knows I can sing every word to "Baby Got Back", and I know he can tie a cherry stem with his tongue. I admit, I spent a few hours picturing that in my head last night.

He hasn't brought up the whole *I dare you to dream about me* comment, and neither have I.

It's Sunday night as I park my Prius at the local Piggly Wiggly and head across the parking lot. I've come to the second grocery store past campus, mostly because I don't want to run into anyone while wearing yoga pants and a sweatshirt with no makeup on. I'm just about to pat myself on the back for not seeing anyone, but that all goes to hell when I'm almost to the door and see Martha-Muffin with one of her sorority girlfriends at the self-checkout near the entrance.

Part of me considers just turning around and leaving. I can always come back later, but once Monday arrives, I tend to be overwhelmed with classes and my job at the library.

Don't let her get the best of you, Delaney.

With my head down, reading the grocery list on my phone, I fortify myself with a mental pep talk and walk through the sliding glass doors.

Don't make eye contact, I tell myself, but before I realize it, I'm glaring right at her. She looks up, catches my eye, and sends me a sly smile, lashes batting.

Our dislike of each other is palpable and always has been. Skye claims she's intimidated and threatened by me because somehow I managed to land a football player as a boyfriend freshman year, and all she got was an STD.

She's wearing her usual, something ridiculous and ill-suited for the cold weather: tall Uggs and a pair of denim shorts lined with lace. Of course, her face is expertly made up, all the way down to the arched eyebrows she probably watched some two-hour YouTube video on how to make.

She finishes checking out and pushes her cart straight over to me, her pert little nose practically twitching with excitement. "Well, well, if it isn't Delaney Shaw." Her gaze sweeps over me, lingering on my baggy Waylon hoodie. "Here to raid the ice cream freezer? Just be careful you don't eat the whole gallon."

I stiffen. As a matter of fact, I do have chocolate ice cream on my list, but it'll be a cold day in hell before I tell her that.

"Don't let me keep you from your Mensa meeting," I say before moving to walk around her.

I've gotten a few feet away when she calls out after me, almost tauntingly. "I can't believe you're being so rude, especially since I haven't seen you in weeks." I cringe, knowing she's referring to the night I caught her with Alex.

I turn back around, knowing I shouldn't, but I just can't stop myself.

She puts a hand on her hip. "Look, you don't have to be so upset about Alex. He's an *athlete*. They screw around—it's what they do."

My stomach churns at the imagery her words bring up, and I feel the blood draining from my face.

Her friend tugs on Martha-Muffin's arm, ushering her out the door, and I stand here for a full five seconds just breathing, trying to get myself under control.

I make my way over to the produce aisle and walk around, not really seeing anything, my heart heavy as I think about Alex and everything we lost.

On an impulse, I pull my phone out of my bag and send a text to my mystery man.

Paging He-Man. I miss you. Where are you? Not that you care, but I'm staring at cherries at the Piggly Wiggly and thinking of you. It's been a shit day. Shit week. Shit month. Just ran into the girl my ex cheated on me with. Need to vent. Need a cigarette…or I would if I smoked.

He replies immediately, and I want to shout with glee.

Awkward. Want me to kick her ass?

Yes.

Done. I'll be there in five.

A laugh comes out of me, and for some reason, seeing Martha-Muffin doesn't have nearly the punch it did a minute ago.

No! I'm just kidding. Plus, she's gone already. Hey, can I ask you a personal question?

Shoot, he replies.

Do YOU sleep with those groupies who hang all over athletes? You know the ones—they've had more loads than a washing machine but they're hot so all the guys want a spin?

Uh…how many loads are we talking?

Of course he sleeps with them. He calls himself "Badass Athlete", and what red-blooded male is going to turn down what's offered?

He-Man, you're disappointing me.

Truth: I haven't been with a girl in months. I'm turning them down left and right.

You're so full of yourself.

True, he says. **But I am the best.**

Best at what? Football? Volleyball? Baseball?

Why are you turning them down? I ask.

I've been waiting on you.

WHAT?

Is he kidding? Is it the truth? He never replies, even after I linger around the produce, waiting to see those three little dots that mean he's responding.

They never appear, and once again I'm overcome with embarrassment at my neediness and lack of male attention. *Screw it.* I stick my phone in my purse and head to the magazine section to pick out a new Cosmo. I move on from there and hit up the meat department. Several minutes later, I'm lifting a large container of ground beef into my cart when I hear a deep male voice behind me.

"Didn't know you liked that much meat, Delaney."

I stop in my tracks.

I turn to see Maverick standing behind me, wearing low-slung jeans, a tight t-shirt, and a grin. We've been sitting together all week in class, and it's been pure torture. We make small talk about the weather and football, but underneath is a current of electricity that I do my best to ignore. Maybe he's ignoring it too.

His gaze brushes over me as if he's undressing me, and a tingling sensation tickles my nose. I can't stop it, sneezing once, twice, three times before I clench my hands together and calm myself.

I'm digging for a tissue in my bag when he says in his southern drawl, "You okay there?"

Sucking in a breath to stop the next one, I hold up a finger for him to give me a minute, and he seems to understand. It would be better if he just moved away.

He takes my packages from me and sets them down in my cart. It's a thoughtful gesture, and I think he does it because he knows he makes me feel out of sorts.

He's just standing there, patiently waiting for me to speak.

"You make me sneeze," I finally say.

"I hope you can find the antidote or we won't be able to hang out together."

"It's worse when I'm surprised by someone, and you're always sneaking up on me." Not exactly true, but I'm making up all kinds of excuses.

"Is it because you think I'm hot, Delaney?"

"Doesn't everyone think you're amazing and wonderful and hot? Been there, done that with a football player, and not doing it again because all it got me was a broken heart."

He rubs at the scruff on his beautifully chiseled jawline. "We're not all cheaters, Delaney."

"I'm not buying it."

He gives me a serious look. "Challenge accepted."

"What challenge?"

"Proving to you that I'm not like anyone you've ever met."

"And how are you going to do that?" I cock my hip and lean against my cart, trying hard to be nonchalant, but it's hard as hell with six feet four inches of solid muscle running his gaze over you.

"You can start by hanging out with me."

"We do…in class."

"No, more than that." He thinks on it, his top teeth chewing on his bottom lip a little. "Definitely somewhere with a lot of other people."

"And why is that?"

He sweeps his gaze over me. "I think we both know what's going to happen if we're alone."

Oh. My. God. He is so infuriatingly arrogant that I can't even…

"I'm not interested in you like that." Total lie. My body definitely is; it's my head that's rebelling.

"Uh-huh." He grins widely.

My eyes flare. "I'm not."

"Are you denying what's going on between us?" His blue eyes are hot as he stares at me, and I might have to step into the ice cream freezer to cool off.

I swallow. "Yes. Flat-out denying."

He shakes his head and laughs a little, his face so self-assured and freaking confident that I want to scream…or kiss him. *What?* Where did that thought come from?

He shuffles his feet. "Maybe I've been waiting two years for you to be free so I could ask you out."

What?!

His eyes go back to the packages of ground beef. He clears his throat. "You never answered my question—what's with all the meat?"

He's changing the subject. *Thank God.* "I cook for the upcoming week on Sunday nights. Monday's taco night, Tuesday's nacho night, and Wednesday is quesadillas."

"She's beautiful *and* she cooks?"

"Stop flirting," I snip. "I'm not beautiful."

"You are."

My body tingles all over at his simple words.

He leans over into my personal space, and I smell him, dark and exotic with a hint of pure male. His finger tilts my chin up until we're staring each other in the face.

I recall the sexy convo with He-Man, about us standing in a cramped bathroom having sex against the wall, only now He-Man has a face and it's Maverick. He's holding me up, cupping my ass as he slides into me, and I'm gasping his name—

I stop, my heart flying as heat rushes to my cheeks. I look down and realize how close we're standing. One more inch and my entire body will be plastered against his, and it's all I can do to stand perfectly still.

Tension crackles in the air as his piercing eyes stare into mine.

"In case you didn't know it already, I like how you look." His eyes slowly drink me in, drifting over my face and lingering on my chest. "All that blonde hair, and your green eyes. I dig how tall you are…and your curves."

Oh, lord. I'm nowhere near as bosomy as most, but I do have nice B-cups.

I'm back in that bathroom fantasy and he's kissing me, his hand on my breast—

I can't breathe.

A soft voice brings us both back to the present. "Mav? I… found…you."

I glance over his shoulder to see a delicate creature with long, flowing russet-colored hair and a heart-shaped face. With creamy, porcelain-perfect skin, she reminds me of the beautiful dolls Nana used to collect. She tilts her head and looks at us with interest.

My lips compress as I turn and mutter under my breath. "You're here with a girl and you're hitting on me?"

Ignoring my comment, he takes a step back and simultaneously reaches out a hand to her. "Hey, I lost you at the candy aisle. You find what you wanted?"

She nods, presenting him with the little carry basket she's hooked on her arm. She shows him a handful of Snickers and a six-pack of Dr. Pepper. "Can...I...have...them?" Her words are drawn out.

I glance back at Maverick to see a soft expression on his face. "You can get them, but you know the rule: only one each per day. Too much of that and..."

She nods. "My...teeth...will...fall...out."

I look from one to the other, thoroughly confused. *Who is she?*

He glances back at me. "Delaney, I'd like you to meet Raven—my sister."

Oh. She does a slow blink then comes toward me, and I notice her leg hitches a bit as she moves. She takes my hand in a limp shake, her expression unsure, as if she's not certain of the etiquette.

"Girlfriend?" she asks, her eyes going from me to him.

Maverick grunts. "Too personal, Raven."

She shrugs and drops my hand, almost sizing me up. "Need...a...girlfriend...so...you...stop...worrying...so... much."

Hmmm. What does Maverick have to worry about?

"Nice to meet you," I say. "And, Maverick and I are just friends."

She squints, looking disappointed. "Oh."

"We have a class together," I tell her.

"Where she mostly ignores me," Maverick adds.

I laugh.

Raven studies me and gives her temple a little tap with her index finger. "Nice…to…meet…you. My…head…is…wonky. I…tell…everyone…so…they…know." She shrugs indifferently.

"Oh, I'm sorry," I say, not quite sure how to respond.

"Don't…be." She smiles sweetly at nothing in particular, her gaze drifting off. "Mav…olives…please?"

He nods. "Of course, get whatever you want. Meet me back at the front to check out, okay?"

She nods, and without another glance at me, moves down the aisle.

I'm watching this in fascination. Maverick has a sister…a sister with special needs…and he adores her—it's obvious in the softness of his eyes as they follow her.

He turns back to me. "What?" he asks, and I guess he's reading my face.

I shake my head. "You're such a surprise."

"Yeah?"

I nod. "Is she the reason the highest-rated defensive player in the country decided to stay home and play for the local college?" It's no secret that Maverick received ESPN's highest ratings and was courted for scholarships from the big schools like University of Alabama and Georgia. I've even heard he promised himself to a big SEC team, but at the last moment decided to stay in Magnolia and play for Waylon—which, admittedly, isn't a horrible team, but it doesn't have the same prestige the Crimson Tide does.

"Yeah. It happened in a car accident my senior year that also took my mom. It…changed a lot of things for me."

His countenance is full of melancholy, an emotion I recognize because I have the same darkness inside of me. Anyone who's lost a loved one knows it. I nod. "I lost my parents at age ten in a car wreck. I get it."

He straightens and gives me a surprised look, almost as if he's restructuring how he sees me. "I never would have known it. You seem so…adjusted."

I huff out a laugh. "Thanks?"

"You know what I mean," he says with a little smirk. "You're a good person, Delaney. You're always kind and sweet and…" He stops talking and shakes his head. "Never mind. I'm talking too much."

I clear my throat, easing over the awkwardness. "Anyway, my Nana took me in and raised me. I'd just graduated high school when she passed from a bad heart. Sometimes I think she waited until I was old enough and then just let go." I don't know what it is about this guy, but suddenly I'm opening up to him.

He nods. "That must have been tough."

I shrug, playing off my grief, but when I look back up, there's this look on his face like he gets me…like he's been there a million times before and—

God.

Stop, Delaney. Just stop. No more football players.

I recall the words Martha-Muffin just spoke to me: *Athletes screw around—it's what they do.*

I clear my throat and move closer to my cart, wrapping my hands around the handle, anchoring myself, because Maverick makes me feel like I might toss aside everything I think about football players and give him a chance. "Look, you're a great guy, and thank you for the offer of hanging out, but it's best if we keep it simple."

He studies me. "You'll change your mind."

My chest rises rapidly, and before I can formulate a snarky reply his sister's voice drifts toward us from down the aisle, calling to him, and he waves back at her.

"Guess I have to run. Later," he says, and then just like that, he's walking off—and *damn* if his ass isn't fine.

I let out a sigh and push my cart to the front to check out.

CHAPTER 6

MAVERICK

"She's...pretty," Raven says as we get in my silver truck, ten-year-old Toyota I bought with my own money when I was sixteen. It's seen its fair share of dings and scrapes, but it still runs like a well-oiled machine. Someday when I'm playing in the NFL, I'll buy something sharp, but for now, I can't think about that. One day at a time is all I can handle.

"Who?" I ask, helping her with her seat belt. Her eyes follow as I clip it into the buckle.

"Have...you...kissed...her?"

Raven's eyes are turned up to me, and the light from the streetlight illuminates her sweet face. Emotion slams into my chest, reminding me that she's not the same, not even close.

"No," I say tersely as I start the truck and drive out of the parking lot.

"You...like...her?"

"Apparently, she's just a friend." I roll my eyes. "This isn't one of your Disney shows where everything has a happily ever after."

She shrugs and looks out the window. "You...should...

ask...her...out."

I shake my head at her, not telling her that I practically had. "Thanks for the dating advice, sis."

Delaney...*where do I even begin with her?* Sure, we met at the bonfire, but I cocked that up, and by the time I tried to find her, she was with Alex. Once a football player has a girl, you can't mess with them. It's the bro code, not to mention the fact that Alex is the kicker and any small thing can freak them out.

I recall the first time I saw her after the bonfire: at a football party, on Alex's arm, looking like she just stepped out of the pages of a geek girl magazine with her glasses, tight jeans, and a *Walking Dead* t-shirt she'd turned into some kind of halter top. What I liked about her was how she never looked at me any different because of who I was. She never put me on a pedestal or kissed my ass. In fact, she always fucking ignored me.

But now she isn't with Alex.

The question is...what am I going to do about it?

I pull up at Dad's doublewide, wishing like hell I had the money to get Raven out of here and in at Pineview Retreat, a state-of-the-art facility near Jackson, Mississippi. I've been eyeing it since she left the home where she was staying.

I put the groceries I bought in the cupboard and wake Dad up. He's fallen asleep watching one of my old high school football games. It brings back memories of when Mom was alive and we were a whole family. Sure, we never had much, not with a dad who couldn't hold down a job and a mom who railed at him constantly, but for me, it had been better than *this*.

He stirs in his recliner and looks up at me with bleary eyes.

Smaller than me with thin shoulders and a haggard face, he's in his fifties but looks older.

"You been drinking?" I ask sharply, feeling more like the parent than the child.

He stands and stretches. "No, just tired. I worked at Bill's today changing oil on some cars he had."

I exhale, staring at him. That's good. As long as he works, everything is fine. I nod. "Just keep it that way."

Dad gets up to make us dinner: leftover meatloaf and potatoes from last night. While he finishes up, I wait outside the bathroom while Raven takes a shower so we can talk through the door. I'm paranoid she'll fall even though her balance has improved. I wish we could afford more than three days a week of a nurse who comes in to do these things.

After dinner, Dad loads the dishwasher and I tuck Raven in her bed. As requested, I make up a random story about a princess and her one true love.

She sighs as I stand up to turn off the light, careful to make sure her butterfly nightlight is still on.

"Mav?"

I pause at the door and hold in my exhalation, not wanting her to see how bone tired I am. I've been going since eight this morning when I hit the gym to box.

"Thank…you."

"You don't have to thank me every time I come see you, goofy."

She sighs. "It's…hard…for…you. Do…me…a…favor?" Her voice is small.

"Anything."

"Kiss…Delaney."

That wasn't what I expected. I thought she'd ask for another cookie from the cupboard or another story.

"Why would I do that?"

She shrugs under the covers as she tucks her chin in, her eyes droopy. "You…just…need…to."

"I'm not sure Delaney wants me to kiss her."

"She…does," she says. "I…have…a…TBI…but…I'm… not…stupid."

I huff out a laugh. "Okay."

"Promise?"

"I promise."

Guess this means I'm kissing her whether it's a good idea or not. I mean, I'd do anything for my sister.

CHAPTER 7

DELANEY

"What you need is a fresh start with a rebound guy," Skye says with a toss of her long red hair as we sit inside Buffalo Bills, a rowdy restaurant and bar near campus. We're in the back in a leather booth, munching on peanuts from a pail as we wait for Tyler and my—*shudder*—blind date to show up. We came a bit earlier than the guys so we could catch up, and so I could get my nerve up with a drink. I haven't been on a date with anyone but Alex since freshman year, and it feels weird.

I take a deep breath. "Tell me more about this Bobby Gene guy—which is a really weird name, by the way."

Bubbly and eager, she waves me off and starts in. "Just ignore his name. You'll love him. He's on the baseball team but not a horn-dog. He's nice—like you requested. No athlete floozies chasing him, no fetishes that I know of."

"Key words being *that I know of.*" I smirk.

"You're just anti-guy right now. At least he isn't a football player."

That is true.

She straightens her red halter top, which matches her hair.

"Plus, Bobby Gene's Tyler's friend, so this is important."

"Of course," I murmur, but I'm feeling ambivalent. I mean, she's put a lot of effort into arranging this, so I don't want to be negative, but...Tyler's a bit of a jerk. I've noticed him checking out other girls when they're together then playing it off when she calls him on it. Maybe it's nothing. Maybe I'm just in a funk because *my* boyfriend cheated on me.

Whatever.

I just hope Bobby Gene is nice.

Skye gets a thoughtful look on her face. "You know, I wanted to tell you that I saw Alex on campus today and he looked...I don't know...sad." She sees my face and holds her hands up. "I mean, yes, he's a major douchebag and I'll hate him until the end of time for you..." Her voice trails off as she grimaces, giving me a *please don't be mad at me* look. "But, I don't know, maybe someday you guys can be friends again?"

I stare down at my drink. That's the rub—we were all three great friends. I also adore Alex's family in Texas, and now I'll never get to see them again. *Ugh.* I don't want to think about him right now.

A noncommittal shrug is my answer.

She sighs. "I'm sorry. I shouldn't have even mentioned it."

I nod. I know she misses him too since he was over at the house a lot. Before she met Tyler, we spent lots of nights hanging out, cooking, and watching movies together. There were even times I was a little jealous of the camaraderie she and Alex had, but I knew she wasn't interested in him that way and he loved me. *Ha. Right.*

Paging Princess Leia. Where are you?

My happiness level goes up a notch as I read the text and quickly tap out a reply. Skye doesn't notice as she orders another round of drinks from our waitress, who's stopped by the table. I don't know why I want to keep He-Man a secret, but I do, as if he's all mine and I need that for some reason.

On a blind date.

Oh. Where?

I'll give you two hints: there are beers and peanuts on the table.

Ah, Buffalo Bills. Do you want me to rescue you? I can call and pretend I'm your aunt who's terribly sick.

I giggle. **That's AWFUL! I'm disappointed you'd encourage a lie.**

Okay. Hey, I saw you at the library last night—nice dare completion. I was digging the buns on your head.

Oh my God. He was there.

My heart thuds, racing back through every single face I encountered.

I recall how at precisely eight, I stood in the middle of the study area and yelled out, "Princess Leia is a badass!" I'd even put my blonde hair up in little fluffy buns on the sides of my head before work. I'd also gone all out with my clothing choices, wearing a fitted white shirt and a pair of white jeans—in February! Deep red lipstick completed the look. If I do a dare, I do it right. The shy girl in me loved letting loose and knowing it was for a dare, which gave me the courage to do it. My eyes scanned the place, but I was so nervous, it was hard to take a good inventory of who was there. It was at least most of the football team since they do study sessions there on Mondays, and several baseball players saw it along with some guys in fraternity jerseys.

Everyone stared. A few clapped. Some whistled.

Did it feel good to do the dare? he asks.

Yes, I reply. It was fucking empowering, especially when Alex stared at me with a forlorn look on his face, obviously missing me.

I saw Maverick there too, surrounded by a group of girls at a table. His response to my outburst? A simple smirk and a head nod.

I chew on my lip, wondering once again who He-Man is.

Hey, you're not the skinny hipster guy who hangs out in the romance section looking for dates are you?

He sends a whole string of laughing/crying emojis.

If I stood in the romance section, I'd never make it out alive. I'm already irresistible, but put Twilight in my hands and girls will piss themselves.

"Why are you giggling?" Skye asks, and I raise my head. Her gaze goes to my phone.

"Just a meme someone sent me," I say as I take a sip of the new beer the waitress apparently set down without me even noticing.

"It must have been a funny one."

"Yeah, it was a cat."

Any mention of my love for cats has her rolling her eyes. She and Han have a love/hate relationship. She gets up and straightens her skirt. "I'm going to head to the ladies' room to freshen up. You'll be okay till I get back?"

I nod. "Sure."

She heads off, and I look back down at my phone as it pings.

Where did you go? Is your date there? Are you riding a bull? Don't ride the bull because I want to be there when you do.

He-Man, I've been thinking...I need to know who you are, I send.

Why? Don't you like being anonymous? Don't you think we're opening up to each other more?

Yes. Maybe. I don't know.

I get nothing but silence in return. My hands clench my phone, waiting to see those telltale little dots, but he isn't responding.

Why doesn't he want to tell me? Is it someone I hate? Is it Alex with a burner phone? Is it Maverick?

I take a deep breath and text, **Are you a football player?**

Yes.

My heart flips over. Is He-Man really Maverick? *God*, I want it to be.

I don't do football players anymore, I text.

You'd do me. It's going to happen.

I squirm in my seat as a bolt of electricity zips through me and my entire body heats up. My skin gets goose bumps, and I know it's because I'm picturing Maverick on the other end of this conversation.

You're cocky, I send, my fingers sweaty.

I know when a woman wants me, and I want you too, Princess Leia. I have for a long time.

I want to ask more, but I'm scared of...*dammit*, I don't

even know. Being hurt? Being lied to?

I spend the next minute staring intently at my phone, trying to think of a response, and I'm still staring when Skye gets back from the restroom. I finally put my phone away when Tyler arrives, along with my blind date.

An hour later, I've met Bobby Gene and we've finished a round of beers and a plate of cheese fries. Handsome with a lopsided grin and cropped brown hair, he's rather engaging. He's made me giggle with his talk of growing up on a pig farm in Iowa, but He-Man is all I can think about.

Each minute I'm here with Bobby Gene feels like an hour, and I'm anxious to get home and text him so we can figure things out.

But is there really anything to figure out?

How can I ever trust a football player again?

My phone rings, surprising me, and I battle down a sneeze when I see He-Man's name on the screen.

"Who's He-Man?" Bobby Gene asks, leaning over and peering down at my phone where I left it sitting on the table.

"Just a friend," I say.

"Well, you gonna get it?" he asks with a grin. He's obviously easygoing and doesn't seem perturbed that I have someone calling me while I'm on a date.

I pick up the phone, excitement curling. "Hello?"

"Hey, I thought you might need a rescue phone call." I can't make out the voice because he's whispering, but it heats every inch of my skin.

I'm talking to He-Man! I want to shout it out to everyone, but that would be weird, so I don't. Instead, I clear my throat, injecting concern into my tone. "Yeah, what's wrong?"

"I've fallen and I can't get up."

I bite my lip to keep from laughing.

"Oh, no. What happened?" I infuse my voice with drama.

"Truth: I was studying and kept thinking about you on your date. Does it suck? Is he ugly? An asshole?"

I glance over at Bobby Gene, who grins.

"No," I say, and I get silence from the other end.

"You mean you like him?" There's an incredulous tone to his voice.

I do like Bobby Gene—as a friend—but I can't answer something so specific with the detail it needs. Too many people are listening to me.

Skye is shooting me a quizzical look, and Tyler is eyeing me suspiciously.

"Uh, yeah? It's great," I answer.

There are several ticks of silence, and I imagine I can feel his unhappiness with my response.

"Are you still there?" I ask, chewing on my bottom lip.

"Yes. I shouldn't have called you. Obviously I've interrupted a good time. Have fun on your date."

Click. He ends the call without even saying goodbye, and I'm surprised.

"I'm so sorry. That's just terrible!" I say to the silence, clutching the phone tighter as I lean over the table. "Yes, of course, I'll go home and call her right away and let you know."

I get off the phone and send a regretful look at Bobby Gene. "Sorry, my aunt is sick—"

"But aren't you from Charlotte?" Tyler asks, a slight curl to his lips. Skye is giving me a pointed look, and I know she knows I'm trying to get out of the date.

I blink. *Oh, God.* Lies truly are a sticky web.

"Yeah, but I just need to check in on her, not actually catch a plane to go see her." I try to sell the lie again. "I should go home and call her." There, it's final: I am a terrible person.

Bobby Gene, bless his heart, gives me a shoulder squeeze, and I feel even worse. "I got 'cha. They don't have to be direct family to be important to you. Maybe we can get coffee and donuts sometime?"

Coffee *and* donuts?

Bobby Gene just went up another notch on my like list.

I agree and we exchange numbers. With a hasty goodbye and a bit of a glare from Skye, I exit Buffalo Bills and head for the house.

It's not until I'm home and lying on the couch with Han on my chest, purring in my ear like a motorboat that I decide to text him.

I'm home, I say.

Alone?

Yeah. You?

Always, he says.

Were you jealous tonight?

Yes.

I stare at the one-word response, my stomach jittery with excitement even though my head is yelling at me that he's a football player.

Biting my lip, I change the topic. **This is random, but do you like cats?**

I'm more of a dog guy.

We can never text again, I quickly type out and send.

Okay, fine, I like them—just for you, Princess Leia.

A pang strikes my heart. He's just…perfect. Everything he says makes me feel fluttery inside, and even though my head is warning me, my heart wants to put a face to the code name of the person I've been texting with.

But for now…I wait.

Good night, He-Man.

As you wish.

CHAPTER 8

DELANEY

Me: If you had a pair of X-ray glasses, what part of my body would you look at first?

He-Man: Collarbone.

Me: LIAR.

He-Man: Fine, fine, you win. I like big tits and I cannot lie. But I do like collarbones too.

Me: Ha. All guys are the same.

He-Man: Fine. What would YOU look at?

Me: I'd look at He-Man's sword, of course.

He-Man: Trust me, it's pretty fucking magnificent.

Me: Wanna send me a pic?

He-Man: Just to clarify, the quiet and reserved Delaney Shaw is asking me for a dick pic?

Me: It sounds bad when you put it like that...

He-Man: I'd rather show you in person, Princess Leia.

Me: Oh.

Can't never could is what my Nana always said and I'm saying that in my head over and over as I shelve books on the third floor a few days later. I'm beat from a long day of volunteering at the cat shelter and now I'm stuck in The Dead Zone of the library, where few roam unless they're doing serious research. At least I have last night's texting with He-Man to think about, which had gotten very sexy before I'd finally let him go.

The next book to shelve is a huge three-inch atlas that weighs a ton. I drag the stepladder from the wall over to the metal shelves so I can reach to the top where it belongs. Once I climb up and clear the shelf, I have a clear view of most of the floor.

I'm about to turn and come down when two guys come up the stairs and onto the third floor, the echoes of their hushed voices carrying across to me. My heart leaps—*damn heart*—when I see Maverick walking next to Ryker, Waylon's quarterback.

Maverick's eyes look up and capture mine—he must have some kind of secret power that detects female attention—and takes me in, hovering above the shelf like a crazy person. He sends me a wave and I smirk.

Ryker taps him on the shoulder to pull his direction toward one of the study areas to the left, but Maverick nods his head at me and walks in my direction. Ryker follows.

Shit! They're coming over.

My hair's in a ponytail and my glasses askew, and I hurriedly pat down the crazy stray strands and straighten my frames. I wish I had time to grab my lipstick, but of course, it's in my purse on the first floor.

"Hey," Maverick says as he turns the corner. He's holding

a book and smiling, looking pleased as punch to see me, and it takes my breath a little.

I blink up at him, taking in the finely carved jawline and bitable lips.

Just. *Damn.*

He's gorgeous and it pisses me off that it makes me melt into a puddle of goo.

I stuff that behind me and give him a nonchalant shrug, keeping my expression easy and not at all like I didn't nearly break my neck getting off the ladder. "Hey."

"You working?"

"Obviously."

His lips twitch. "You sound excited."

"I'm not. What are you doing here?" I ask.

"Just roaming the library."

"Why?"

He tilts his head, studying me. "Why not?"

"It's a bit late for mind games, Maverick." I look down at the cart full of books I still have to shelve. "And I have work to do."

"Maybe I was looking for you. I can help if you want?"

My eyes flare. *Damn.* Why does he have to be so sweet sometimes? "That's okay."

He gazes around at the shelving, taking in the empty tables and then focuses back on me. "This would be a great place to hook-up. Ever consider it?"

I roll my eyes. "Scoping out future make-out places? Please, for the sake of the books, leave the library out of your pound town itinerary."

He throws up a cocky eyebrow. "I like the dim lighting and all the shelves. Good coverage in case someone comes up."

My face colors, picturing him with some pretty co-ed.

He grins. "Would you be jealous if I hooked up with someone here?"

"No, don't be ridiculous," I say. *Yes.*

He studies me, eyes at half-mast. "Okay, fine, Delaney. I'll never hook-up with anyone in the library…unless it's you."

My mouth opens and I'm about to say something *really* witty and smart—although I can't think of a damn thing—when Ryker turns the corner. I guess something must have caught his eye on the way over and that's why he lagged behind.

Obviously, Maverick has impeccable timing.

The quarterback gives me a nod. "Ah, Delaney. Surprise, surprise."

Is he being facetious?

Because he doesn't sound surprised. He sounds cryptic and a little pleased with himself if that makes sense. I squint at him, reminding myself to play back this conversation later.

"Hey, Ryker," I say, giving him a nod. "We rarely get people on the third floor, so…welcome?" I hold my hands out.

Ryker looks around. "Yeah. It's dead up here. Great place for a hook-up."

I shake my head. "Oh my God. Is that all guys think about?"

"Yeah," they say in unison.

"Typical," I say with a laugh.

Almost as if he knows I'm putting up my internal defenses

against him, Maverick takes a step closer and picks at a spot on the shoulder of my black shirt. Butterflies take off inside me as his index finger and thumb press together on the fabric to grab a white hair.

"What's this?" he asks.

Swallowing, I look down at his hand and clear my throat. "Cat hair. I got in the kitten tent today at the shelter and they crawled all over me. Super adorable. I'd love to bring one home but Han would flip his lid."

Ryker takes a full two steps back from me, his eyes wide. "You rolled around with cats?"

"Well, not literally, but yeah. It's very therapeutic. Are you allergic?"

He nods.

"That's awful." I grimace.

He waves me off. "No worries. I'll just stand over here so I don't breathe it in. That way you guys can chat." He finds a spot about ten feet away and pretends to look at a book. I say *pretend* because it's a reference book about rivers in South America and I can't imagine why he'd be interested, but who knows.

It's almost as if they planned on seeing me...

I turn back to Maverick who hasn't taken his eyes off me. "I'm completely non-allergic to cats," he tells me.

"Why should I care?" I'm being bratty, but his cockiness brings it out in me.

He isn't fazed and plucks another hair off me, this time around the neckline of my shirt. His fingers brush my collarbone and I inhale sharply, remembering the texting convo about collarbones with He-Man. "You're really covered in these." My chest rises rapidly, and he grins, leaving me convinced the man is the devil.

I'm saved just as I hear Skye talking. We'd made plans to meet after my shift and grab a drink at Buffalo Bills before we head home. She's probably on her way up here to keep me company until I'm done.

I hear her talking to someone as she calls out my name rather tentatively, which is odd, and I'm wondering who's with her. It sounds like a guy, but not Tyler...

Alex and Skye appear from around the corner of the shelf and I start, stiffening.

What the hell is she doing with him?

With a sheepish expression on her face, she clears her throat and waves at everyone. "Hey, y'all."

I'm frowning as my gaze goes from her to Alex.

She nods, reading my expression. "Ah, yeah. Alex saw me on the staircase on my way up and wanted to talk..." Her voice drifts off.

Ah, I fill in the rest. She couldn't tell him to buzz off. She's too nice and she'd probably done her best to dissuade him.

Alex's eyes are measuring the space between Maverick and me, which admittedly is just a few inches.

"What are you doing up here?" he asks Maverick.

Maverick straightens, his back going stiff. "It *is* the library. People do come here to study. What are *you* doing here?"

Alex taps his hand against his thighs and juts out his jaw. "Studying. Same as you."

"I don't see any books, kicker," Maverick says.

A spot of red appears on Alex's cheeks. "I left them on the first floor—since you're so interested."

"Huh. Maybe you should go get them."

Alex's face hardens. "Why? Am I interrupting anything between you and Delaney?"

Jesus take the wheel. They are both crazy.

I hold my hands up. "Hang on a minute—"

"Yeah," Ryker says, interrupting me. He's put down the reference book and has joined us, his brow pulled low in a scowl as he takes in the back and forth between the two. "We don't need any trouble here, guys."

Skye takes Alex by the arm. "Why don't we head back downstairs?"

Alex pulls his gaze from Maverick and looks down at her, a slight softening in his face. "Sure. Sounds good." He sends me a resigned expression. "Bye, Delaney."

They turn to go and Skye gives me an *I'm sorry* look over her shoulder as they walk away.

"Dude. Not cool or subtle," Ryker says to Maverick as soon as they are out of earshot. "Did you have to be a dick?"

Maverick's nose flares. "He was a dick first."

"Yeah, but you're a leader," Ryker tells him. "The team needs you to show everyone else how to act."

Maverick lets out a long exhale, his hand rubbing at the back of his neck. "Yeah."

Hang on a minute. Maverick is jealous of Alex? I'm about to remark on it, but he brushes past me, his tall frame stalking off. Part of me wants to call him back, but pride and all.

I look at Ryker and raise my hands up. "What's going on?"

"If you can't see what's right in front of you…" He shrugs. "Later, babe."

And then he's walking off but not before turning around for one more comment. "Just do me a favor, okay? Don't hurt him. He's been through enough already."

My heart drops at the thought of hurting Maverick. Of course I wouldn't.

CHAPTER 9

DELANEY

The cafeteria in the student center is loud with the sounds of clanging dishes and students' voices. I'm not here to eat, just to grab a soda before I head upstairs to my first salsa lesson.

I get to the register, pay for my Coke, and then head for the exit. My eyes can't help but wander to the far left corner table near the windows where the football players usually sit in a huddle. I come to a stop when blue eyes meet mine. A flash of awareness washes over me as Maverick rakes his gaze up and down.

A small smile tilts up the side of his mouth, and it infuriates me that he seems to *know* he makes my body do crazy things. He'd acted jealous of Alex in The Dead Zone a few days ago but neither of us has mentioned it since. I guess we've decided to let it go.

Miss Brunette—the same one from class—approaches his table and plops down in the seat next to him. Her hands snake around his bicep as she looks up at him adoringly.

I feel the eye roll coming, and instead of stopping myself, I let him see it.

There you go, folks: further proof that football players are magnets for floozies.

I tip my soda at him and he smirks, as if saying, *I can't help it if women love me.*

You're so full of shit, my face says back.

He gives me a full-blown grin before looking over at her with that distant smile, the one I know isn't authentic. He leans in and says something to her, and she looks crestfallen.

He turns back to me and stands.

He mouths something, and it looks like *Wait for me.*

I glance around to make sure he means me, and the only person near me is a cafeteria worker in a white jumpsuit. Looking back at him, I point to myself, just to confirm.

He nods and makes his way along the tables, weaving through players and girls and the general maze that is our cafeteria.

My body draws up in anxiety. I'm not ready to deal with Maverick and his intensity, so I do what I do best.

I bolt.

I have somewhere to be anyway.

Flipping around with a flounce of my ponytail, I head for the exit in a full-on speed walk that's debatably a run. I clear the door and dart for the elevator to head up to the third floor.

As soon as I exit, I approach the door to the dance studio. From inside, I hear the low undertones of a conga drum and maracas, so I know I'm at the right place. On the door hangs a sign that says *Welcome to Salsa 101! Can't dance? We can change that!* I hope that isn't a lie. I'm fascinated with Latin music and food, and learning to salsa is on my bucket list...

hence the urge to finally show up when I don't even have a partner.

I open the door to the studio, which is actually just a room on the third floor of the student center. In my hand is the flyer that lists the class times and requirements along with the twenty dollars to cover the cost of the lessons.

I'm tempted to text He-Man and tell him what I'm doing, to see if he'd be proud of me for coming alone. I make a mental note to take a selfie and send it to him later.

It's a large square-shaped room with a sound system in the corner and an entire wall covered in mirrors. My eyes scan the space and land on a tall, thin male wearing super tight black pants and a red sequined shirt. He's sitting at a small table in the corner, next to the sound system. Dark gelled hair is brushed straight up from his forehead, and there might be the sparkle of shimmery eye shadow on his lids. I catch a small white nametag pinned to his shirt that reads *Ricardo, Dance Instructor.*

I'm definitely in the right place.

He looks up from his clipboard and brushes his gaze over me. "Here for salsa?" He looks past me. "Alone?" I can hear the surprise in his tone.

"Um, yes," I say, forcing conviction and confidence into my voice. I really do want this. "Is that okay?"

A doubtful look crosses his face. "Typically, it works best if you have a partner. Everyone else has a partner. I might be able to jump in and dance with you, but I'm usually too busy."

Nice. Even the teacher doesn't want to dance with me.

A group of people standing next to a refreshment table a

few feet over swivel their heads as his voice carries over to them.

"Right, I saw that in the flyer. Normally my roommate would jump at the chance to do this, but well, she's got this new boyfriend. I mean, who doesn't want to learn to salsa…" My voice peters out and I sigh as I realize I'm rambling.

Ricardo gives me a wry yet kind smile. "Ideally you learn how the rhythm of the body works when you have someone to mirror the moves with you."

I push my glasses up on my nose and shuffle my feet, thinking I should have just stayed at home and watched a movie.

The instructor gets distracted as another couple comes in the door, and I ease off to the side, looking for the nearest exit.

Could I leave without anyone noticing?

I pause, clenching my fists.

Why do I care so much? So what if I'm alone?

Where are your balls, Delaney? WHERE ARE THEY?

I dare myself to go through with it.

I slap my money down on the table and Ricardo turns back toward me, a surprised expression on his face as he takes in my crossed arms. "I'm here to have fun with or without a partner, and who's to say I might not start a new trend: salsa sans partner. You never know, it could be the next big thing in ballroom dancing."

Ricardo's face breaks into a smile as he swishes around the table to hand me a nametag to put on my shirt. "I like your spirit," he says as I scrawl my name on it with a pen and slap it on my *Game of Thrones* shirt. I'm here and I'm ready to rumble.

Bobby Gene appears in front of me. "What! Are you kidding me? Delaney Shaw comes to salsa lessons?" He grins broadly and I automatically give him a hug. With his brown hair and soft eyes, he has an infectious personality that puts me at ease.

"I'm just here for the great Cuban food," he whispers conspiratorially as he nods his head at the long table filled with various dishes and small bottles of water. "And a girl I work with at the school paper. She roped me into this, and I couldn't say no." He points out a perky little redhead with freckles, and she waves at me enthusiastically.

"Where's your partner?" he asks.

"Don't have one," I say.

"Really?" He looks confused. "But how will you—"

"I'm her partner," says a deep voice behind me, and I know who it is before I even turn around.

A sneeze racks my body—of course.

I battle down the next one and turn to face him.

Maverick stands before me like some kind of Greek god, with his lush lips, magnificent body, and perfect blond hair perfectly swept back. My mouth dries as I take in the fitted black shirt that clings to his sculpted muscles. Does the man ever have a bad hair day or *anything*?

"What on earth are you doing in here?" I whisper-hiss, although I don't really have to because Bobby Gene has taken one look at Maverick's glare and wandered back to his partner.

"Honestly, I was following you. Had no clue it was to a dance class...but now that I'm here, I may as well help you out. I heard you don't have a partner." He cocks his head, waiting for my reply. "I must warn you though…I can't dance."

I shrug, trying to play it cool when on the inside I'm a mess, quivering with excitement that he's here…with me. "Well, I am alone, and so are you, and apparently the food is great here. Want to check it out before we get started?"

He grins. "You're asking a football player if he wants to eat? I just had dinner—as you know, since you ran away from me—but lead the way, my lady."

He gives me his arm and I take it.

We make our way over to the table, which is stocked with dishes that have little placards next to each one, naming the contents. I take in the marinated olives, fancy cheeses, fried plantains, and flan.

"Wow. If I had known all this was here, I might have tried this a lot sooner," I say.

Maverick picks up a ramekin of flan and hands me one. "Let's try this."

He gets his own and we each take a bite at the same time, our eyes closing in simultaneous ecstasy.

"Damn, that's good," he says, his eyes on my face instead of the caramel pastry.

"It is," I reply as I watch him savor the bite.

I'm relieved when the instructor claps his hands and motions for us to move to the center of the room.

Disposing of our dishes, we follow his directions.

Ricardo's eyes widen as he takes Maverick in and then he looks at me, a little smile on his face. "I see you found a partner after all, Miss Shaw. Nice choice."

"Indeed," I say.

Maverick smirks and shrugs.

Ricardo goes on to explain that the salsa attitude comes from the music, the dance is something you feel with your body, and at the same time, your brain can memorize the mechanics of the eight-count method. He's enthusiastic as he runs through the steps around the circle we're standing in. I try to pay attention but it's difficult with Maverick standing next to me, our arms brushing against one another.

"First, we must start with the embrace," Ricardo says, pulling on the arm of a tiny woman in a matching red dress who I assume is his partner. He pulls her close with a twirling motion and stares deep into her eyes. "You hold them with intense emotion. You're going on a journey of love and you must convey this in your every movement, in your eyes, in the sensuality of your muscles as you hold your partner tight."

I need a fan just from his words. Ricardo is quite the romantic.

He demonstrates by leaning in and putting his left hand on her shoulder. He hugs her tight then wraps his right arm around her lower back, centering it above her ass. His partner then raises her right hand to mirror his movements.

"Keep your head high, your spine straight, your core strong, and your chest lifted. Ooze confidence, my loves!" Ricardo demonstrates with a sliding movement of his feet as he twirls his partner around. "Move forward with your left foot, then forward with your right, forward with the left, then the right. Then, feet together, moving left to meet right. Tada! That's it, and repeat!" He stops and takes a little bow along with his partner who, of course, mirrored his movements while moving backward. He claps his hands. "Now, let's partner up and hold each other with deep sensuality."

Sensuality?

I turn to face Maverick, a small laugh escaping me. "Are you as uncomfortable as I am right now?"

"I don't have a clue what the hell he just did out there." He grins in a self-deprecating way, a spot of pink on his cheeks.

"Does that embarrass you? That you can't do everything?"

"No, but I do want to make a good impression on you."

My heart does a somersault.

"Why?"

He ignores that comment and pulls me into his arms, his left hand on my shoulder and his right going to the base of my spine. Goose bumps rise on my arms as he tugs me in closer. "Put your arms around me."

I do, my mouth completely dry, my body in tune and ready to catch fire as his chest grazes against me and his leg fits smoothly between mine. Heat engulfs my lower regions and I ignore it by staring at his chin. I can't bring myself to look into those eyes.

"I'd do anything for some people—you'll figure that out about me," Maverick says softly, and suddenly it feels as if we're all alone and not in a crowded studio surrounded by people.

"So I'm one of those people? We barely know each other."

A bit of a laugh comes from him as our eyes meet. "You pretend like you don't know me, Delaney, but there's something between us."

I bite my lip and stammer out, "I have no idea what you're talking about. Plus, I don't like football players."

"So you keep saying, yet here we are...dancing."

"You offered, and I didn't have anyone else."

He laughs. "You love being in my arms and you know it."

I narrow my eyes at him. "You're so freaking infuriating."

He just shrugs.

"I'm not changing my mind."

He leans in and whispers in my ear. "Your body already says *yes*."

Oh...God! He's so annoying, but dammit if his proximity isn't creating havoc in my internal organs, and it's all I can do to not straddle his leg and hump it. Luckily, I'm saved when he begins the forward motion of his feet and I take a step back to mirror his steps.

It's pure torture the way he guides me across the dance floor, his hold firm yet loose, his movements fluid and graceful. He's not as horrible a dancer as he said, and I feel like he only said that to make me comfortable.

Later, after the class is done, we're standing near the door talking as the students mill around and Ricardo ushers everyone out the door.

Bobby Gene gives us a wave as he passes us in the hallway. He looks like he might want to say more, but he gives Maverick a wide berth and calls over his shoulder that he'll catch me later.

We decide to take the stairs instead of the elevator since it's packed. Maverick walks next to me, his body solid and hard, and I'm feeling more powerful than I have in days.

"Want me to walk you to your car?" he asks as we reach the bottom floor.

"Uh, yeah, sure."

Even though there are plenty of streetlights and security cameras, it is dark.

We walk toward the exit, but then I see Martha-Muffin watching us from a cozy sitting area off to the right. Her eyes are lasered in on Maverick and then they bounce to me, a slight snarl forming on her face. I must slow or stiffen because Maverick pauses and looks down at me. "You okay?"

I take a deep breath and shake my head. "It's nothing."

A scowl forms on his brow as he scans the open space of the lobby, his gaze landing on Martha-Muffin, who's put her hand on her hip, openly glaring at us.

"Ah, her…" He stops and looks back at me with a grimace. "If it's any consolation, I can't stand her. She tried to trick her way into my bed once and I kicked her ass out. She's been hating on me ever since."

I can't imagine anyone hating Maverick, and I'm glad he's never been with her. But, seeing her just reminds me of Alex's infidelity and the fact that while Maverick hasn't been with her specifically, he's still a football player with plenty of access.

We exit the building and take off across the parking lot. I'm wondering if he'll ask me out again. What will I say? Am I still on this *just friends* kick?

We reach my silver Prius and he grins. "The kind of car you have says a lot about a person."

"Is this where you say I'm pragmatic and predictable?"

He stares down at me. "Maybe. I like that about you.

You're quiet but deep. I am too. I mean, I'm popular but underneath, I'm a quiet guy."

I bite my lip, wanting to know more. "What would you do if you didn't play football?" I ask.

He sticks his hands in his pockets and stares up at the sky as he thinks. "Medical school, probably a neurologist."

Ah. "Because of Raven?"

He smiles ruefully, a contemplative look on his face. "Yeah. I read everything I can about her injury, all the latest findings. It's a complex condition, and very...personal. No two cases are ever the same. Her injuries were rather serious. She had to learn to talk and walk all over again."

"You're a good brother."

He shrugs. "She's all I have. I mean, there's my dad, but sometimes I think he's already given up."

I inhale a sharp breath at his vulnerability. There's so much more to him than everyone thinks.

We stare at each other in silence, and it's not weird or uncomfortable, and...

I'm dying for him to kiss me.

His gaze brushes over me, lingering on my lips. "Want to do the salsa thing again next week?"

"Yeah."

God.

I really want him to kiss me.

Which is crazy. He's bad news...right?

He leans down and brushes his sensuous lips across mine, and for three seconds, I can't breathe.

My body hums. My heart flies. We feel connected, as if his

lips on mine were always meant to be but we're just now figuring it out.

"Our second kiss," he says softly, pulling back to stare down at me.

"Yeah."

"It won't be the last," he says huskily, his voice sending shivers over my skin.

Then he takes my keys from me, opens my door, and helps me inside. He waits as I start the car and drive away.

The entire trip home is a blur because all I can think about is him.

What am I going to do about Maverick Monroe and how he makes me feel?

CHAPTER 10

DELANEY

Me: Did you see tonight's episode of Game of Thrones? OMG.

He-Man: Yep. Now I want a pet dragon.

Me: Would you settle for a cat?

He-Man: Only if you come with it.

"I can't believe you talked me into this party," I mutter to Skye Friday night as I walk next to her up the sidewalk as we make our way to the baseball frat house near campus. It isn't really a frat at all, just a huge colonial brick house donated by one of the former players from Waylon who went on to play major league baseball.

"Well, you need to get out of the house. Plus, that outfit is amazing and we can't waste it." She eyes the black asymmetrical knit mini-dress I'm wearing. I spent my free time this week piecing together and sewing it. Made of jersey, it's formfitting with a band of thick cream lace on the bottom, giving it a flounce. The neckline has little hearts cut out of the fabric while the back is cut into strips, creating a peekaboo effect.

"You're so talented," she murmurs. "Instead of being a graphic designer, you should consider fashion."

I laugh. "Ha. Me?"

"You'd rock a nerd girl line. Think about it: cute little up-cycled dresses, shirts with books on them…the possibilities are endless."

I shrug. Skye is sweet, but I'm not sure I'm fashion material. I just like being different and wearing something no one else has.

"Oh my God, I'm having so many epiphanies tonight." She grabs my arm and stops walking. "Text your He-Man and see if he wants to meet you there!"

Yes, I ended up telling her about him one night this week when I'd had a few glasses of wine.

I nibble on my lips. "I kinda like not knowing who he is. It's…freeing."

She thinks. "True, but wouldn't it be great to have a guy with you in case Alex is at the party?"

"He probably will be." The jocks tend to stick together.

My brain mulls it over, part of me scared. He-Man and I have such great conversations. What if it's not Maverick—the person I really want it to be—but some pimply-faced water boy?

Skye sighs. "You know what, stop thinking about why you shouldn't. Just do it."

"Fine." I pull out my phone and type: **I need you, He-Man.**

Ten seconds go by and I don't see him replying, so I send another text.

I'm still single, in case you were wondering.

Still nothing.

I'm headed to the baseball party. Do you want to meet me there?

"What's he saying?" Skye asks.

I shake my head. "Nothing. He's playing hard to get."

She takes my phone, reads through the messages, and before I can stop her, she's typing out another one.

I'm a little drunk, a lot horny, and all alone. Come with me to the party, and I mean really COME.

She hands it back to me in triumph.

"I don't think that message is *quite* slutty enough," I say with a smirk.

Skye laughs then shouts as the three little dots appear. "Well it worked—he's replying!"

Already here, Princess Leia. Remember the first night we texted? The fantasy of us at a frat party?

My heart flutters.

Yes, I text back. It's never far from my mind.

Meet me upstairs in the bathroom in an hour and we'll make it come true. I dare you.

Excitement steals my breath at the thought of seeing him for real, but are we really going to hook up? I swallow. **How will I know it's you?**

I'll be the only badass athlete waiting for you in the bathroom.

My hands are trembling as I tuck my phone back in my clutch and look at Skye. "Shit. He's here and we're going to meet in the bathroom."

Skye claps, giddy for me. "You're going to have sex," she sings.

"It doesn't mean that," I say, trying to shush her as we approach the door to the house, but I have to admit the exhilaration is making my steps light as we make our way inside.

I get to see He-Man!

The room is packed with groups of people talking and drinking or making out in corners. Loud music blares from the sound system, and I estimate the drunk factor is already at a five on a scale of one to ten.

Tyler calls out from the hallway where he's chatting with some other baseball players, his hand waving at us to come over. Skye gives me a questioning look. "Want to come with?"

I shake my head. "You go on. I'll find the bar."

She heads off toward Tyler, and I watch as she jumps at him. He catches her in his arms and lays one on her.

Bobby Gene calls out my name, and I look up to see him standing upstairs. He's looking handsome with a ball cap on and his arm tossed around the redhead from dance class. "Delaney!" He tips his beer at me.

I tilt my head toward his beer. "I need one of those—stat."

Someone jostles into me from behind, and I turn to see Maverick. He runs his eyes over me, lingering on the cutouts on my chest.

Goose bumps pop up on my skin. I'm hyperaware of every single nerve ending in my body when he's near.

"So are you always bumping into people or is that just me?" he says.

"You bumped into me," I retort with a grin. "It's like you were waiting for me."

Was he?

He shrugs, those broad shoulders shifting with an animalistic grace. He's wearing a fitted orange and blue Wildcats shirt that hugs his chest, the sleeves tight around his hard biceps.

I get distracted when my eyes go past him and I see Alex with Martha-Muffin trailing along behind him. He looks annoyed, and her eyes are red as if she's been crying. I study them more intently, taking in the sad expression she wears as she stares longingly at Alex. I don't really want to know what's going on between them, but it's apparent she really likes him.

I inch in closer to Maverick, needing to get away from them. "Why don't you show me the bar in this place? Isn't it in the back room?"

As if reading my mind, he tosses a glance over his shoulder and sees Alex. He looks back and gives me a nod. "Done."

CHAPTER 11

MAVERICK

We're sitting on a couch in the back room. People come and go past us, mostly on their way outside where the fire pit is, yet it feels like we're alone. She's all I can see right now, and I've been counting down the days until I can go to a damn salsa lesson with her again. *Fuck me, I want Delaney Shaw.*

I never imagined I'd be this…*intense* about wanting a girl, but here I am. Something about her has me worked up, has me wanting everything I never thought I did.

She smiles at me, her ruby lips curving. "So, let's go back to freshman year—why exactly did you kiss me?"

"Because of the legend. The first person you kiss at your first bonfire at Waylon is the one you'll never forget."

She leans into me. "But you *did* forget about me. You went home with twins."

"Whom I barely remember." I exhale, thinking back to how I was at eighteen. "The truth is, I didn't know what I wanted back then. Plus, the accident had just happened a few months before. My head wasn't in the right place."

"And it is now?"

"I'm not perfect, but I know what I want." My eyes go heavy as I run my gaze over her, taking in the way her breasts push against the fabric of her dress. "You're the one that got away, Delaney, the opportunity I missed."

My hand goes to her back and strums across the bare skin of her shoulder. Her skin feels like silk, soft and velvety.

"And you think you can just sweet-talk me into giving another football player a chance?"

I grin. "Yes."

A little laugh comes from her. "Sometimes I'd like to just slap you."

I smirk. "That means I have an effect on you."

"You drive me crazy," she murmurs, her eyes going low.

Our faces are closer now, and her scent washes over me, light and fresh, like lemons.

I touch her face, tracing the line of her jaw.

"What are you doing?" she asks, her voice whisper soft.

"I'm going to prove that this heat between us…it's got to be dealt with," I say.

"Why?"

"Because I can't sit by you in class one more day without doing something about it."

Just before I'm about to press my mouth to hers, someone barks out my name.

CHAPTER 12

DELANEY

He's going to kiss me...until he doesn't, his head turning sharply at the sound of his name.

Anger clouds his face, and I look over to see Alex and Ryker and several other football players striding toward us. Suddenly the room seems full of people swiveling their heads in our direction. Maverick stands, and I do the same. Martha-Muffin is here too, huddled in the corner with some of her sorority sisters, her eyes darting from me to Alex.

I stiffen my shoulders and tilt my chin up as he stops in front of us, his eyes bouncing from me to Maverick. Ryker trails behind him, a worried expression on his face as he looks at Maverick.

"Everything okay here?" Alex says, his chest rising rapidly. A muscle ticks in his jaw.

Maverick towers over Alex, his body coiled like a snake, his face tight. "She's fine. Why are you asking?"

"One of the freshmen said you were getting cozy with Delaney," he snaps. "That isn't cool—not at all."

Maverick scowls and takes several steps away from me,

forcing Alex to move backward. In a matter of seconds, the space between us has been filled by other players surrounding them, waiting to see what's going to happen.

"You aren't dating her. What's the problem?" Maverick bites out.

"The problem is I know *you* aren't Delaney's style, and I wanted to check on her. Besides, it's a shitty guy that hits on a teammate's ex."

I've pushed my way through the throng of people and I see Alex crossing his arms. His face is red with anger.

Shit. This is escalating fast.

Maverick inhales a deep breath, his fists clenching. "That's up to her. She can make up her own mind."

Ryker steps in between them, his voice low. "Hey, hey, look, this is just a little misunderstanding. No one is angry here. Everything is cool."

Some of the other players grumble out an agreement, but neither guy seems to be listening.

Maverick's eyes have narrowed in on Alex. "There's no misunderstanding. I was sitting with Delaney. Everything was fine until he showed up."

Alex puffs up his chest. "She still cares about me, and you're just getting in the way."

Maverick bristles and leans his face into Alex's. His index finger pushes at Alex's chest, forcing him to take a step back. If a fight is about to happen, it's clear who would win. "Stay out of *my way*, kicker, or you'll regret it."

Alex pales and is fumbling for a response when Maverick spins on his heel and stalks out the back door into the yard. I exhale, watching him go.

I should let him cool off.

But I don't. I head out the door, chasing him to the back gate that connects to the front drive.

"Maverick! Wait."

He halts and flips around to face me, his jawline taut with repressed anger. There's about ten feet between us, but I can read him like a book. He's coiled like a tiger, ready to spring.

His gaze brushes over me, and I think I see a flash of regret flicker across his face.

"Delaney…go back inside."

I lift my hands up. "Why? Where are you going?"

He exhales slowly as he sticks his hands in his pockets. "I just need to cool off, okay?" His eyes flick back to the house. "I can't go back in there. I'm on the verge of kicking Alex's ass, and I can't do that."

Oh.

I get it—he wants to flirt with me, but I'm not quite important enough to go against his teammates for.

Fine. Football is king, and nothing else matters.

Disappointment hits me. "So you're just giving up?"

His lips flatten and he doesn't meet my gaze. "Later," he says, and then he's walking away from me.

I stalk back into the house, my hands clenched, disappointment churning. Part of me is…hurt. Just when I'd been softening to the idea of a football player, he goes and blows me off.

It's been almost an hour, so I decide to go upstairs and meet He-Man. Careful to avoid Alex, I head upstairs to the hallway to wait outside the bathroom while a myriad of people come and go.

I'm anxious to see He-Man, but when he's fifteen minutes late, I'm starting to look like a bathroom stalker. I pull out my phone.

I'm here and you're not. Are you standing me up?

No reply.

You suck, I send, typing the words.

I can't make it, he replies. **Sorry. Something came up.**

My stomach drops as I suck in a breath. Why is everyone letting me down?

Feeling more devastated than I should about a guy I've just been texting with, I shove my phone back into my clutch.

Alex is a cheating dick, Maverick ditched me, and now He-Man is a no-show.

All men are jerks.

CHAPTER 13

MAVERICK

"I'm sorry I had to call you to come get him," Mick says as I march up to the counter of a local bar, aptly named *Mick's*. It's a rather seedy, dusty place that plays old country songs, and it's my father's favorite, even though he's been kicked out of it at least half a dozen times that I know of.

My hands clench. I didn't see Mick's voicemails until two hours after he left them because of football practice.

"What happened?" I ask, looking around and assessing, not seeing Dad or Raven. It's a Monday evening and the place is dotted with a few worn faces.

His head nods to a back booth and my eyes follow, landing on my father. "He's been here drinking since six. He fell pretty hard and hurt his hand. Nothing too serious, I don't think, but Jackie played nursemaid back in the office." I see the large white bandage. "He begged me not to call you, but I knew you'd want to know."

Anger curls inside me. "Where's Raven?" I ask, my eyes scanning the room once again.

"In the office with Jackie." Mick sends me a sympathetic

look. "Look, I know things are busy at school, but something needs to be done."

My entire body tightens. "I'm doing the best I can."

What I don't tell him is that I'm driving out to the trailer multiple times a week to take care of her, even though it's half an hour from campus. In a perfect world, I'd just move back in with Dad and Raven, but Coach Al requires us to live in the dorms.

I deal with my dad first, walking over to his booth and shaking his shoulder. "Dad!"

He reeks of bourbon and stale cigarettes, making bile rise up in my throat. It's a smell I recall from my early days as a kid, coming home from school to see him passed out on the couch.

"Mav," he slurs, raising his head up as spittle slides out of his mouth. "I'm sorry...didn't mean to...all my fault." The words are low and barely decipherable through the whiskey.

"I can't believe you brought Raven here," I snap, my gaze brushing over the patrons at the bar. "*Anything* could have happened to her."

"Didn't have money for a sitter." His eyes blink up at me, bloodshot and runny with a wetness I don't want to decipher. *I don't care*, I tell myself.

"You're a son of a bitch," I mutter as I lean down and pull him to the edge of the booth so I can swoop him up in my arms.

His chin falls down to his chest.

I brush past the bar and carry him out the front door. Ryker is waiting for me, his arms crossed against his chest. Same as me, he's dressed in workout clothes, and he straightens up from leaning against my truck. Normally I wouldn't have asked him to come down here with me, but he was with me when I listened to the voicemails. I motion for him to open the door so I can prop Dad up in the backseat.

He watches me with a grim face, his gaze brushing over my father. "What the hell? Shit," he mutters.

With a withering glare at my dad's lowered head, I head back inside with Ryker following me.

Mick ushers me to the back office and we sweep inside. Raven is sitting in a recliner watching *Family Feud*, her face pale and her cheeks stained with tears. Jackie is sitting at the desk working on a laptop, and she gives me a soft nod and a pat on the shoulder. "She's okay, love, just feeling out of sorts."

"Mav!" Raven lights up as she rushes over to me.

She bursts into tears as she jumps toward me, her thin arms wrapping around my shoulders. *God, I need to do better by her.*

"I'm sorry. I never dreamed he'd bring you here."

Cupping my face, she searches my eyes then gives a little knock to her head. "I…have…headache."

I kiss the top of her head. "Come on, Rav. I got you. Let's get you home."

Later that night as Ryker and I drive back to campus, my head is wrecked, riddled with worry and trying to come up with a solution. Only one thing is certain: I want Raven out of my dad's trailer.

The problem is, I don't have the money to fund it. I can't ask for a loan from Coach or *anyone* at school, and I can't have a job that pays over two thousand dollars; those rules are in place to prevent bribing and payouts. My dad has zero credit, so he's out as well.

Ryker keeps shooting me careful looks and I know he's worried about me, which is funny considering this past weekend he was worried I was causing trouble for the team with Delaney. Obviously, I have bigger issues right now.

Once we get back to the dorms, I give him a brusque good night then go into my bedroom and dig around in my nightstand for the number the casino owner gave me.

I recall his offer to pay me money—a lot of money—to fight another football player.

He answers on the first ring.

"Hello?"

"Mr. Leslie Brock?"

"Yes? Who's this?"

I clear my throat, picturing the sharp-toothed, plump man who was at Carson's Gym. "This is Maverick Monroe from Waylon. You made me an offer a few months back when we bumped into each other at Carson's Gym?"

"Ah, yes, the famous football player. You have quite the record, young man."

Whatever. I know he's just a bull-shitter. "Are you still interested?"

"Hmmmm," he says, as if thinking long and hard, and I clench the phone. I mean, he should be fucking *thrilled* I called him. I know the deal he's running, and it's sketchy as hell. I'm a damn fine player and he'd be crazy—

"Can you come to Carson's next week? We can finalize the details there and I can tell you more about the fight."

I exhale. "Sounds good. Text me the day and time and I'll be there."

There's a tone of satisfaction in his tone when he replies. "Excellent. You won't regret this, Maverick."

I tap my screen to end the call.

I'm already regretting it, but I don't see any other options.

CHAPTER 14

MAVERICK

The next day Raven and I drive out to Pineview Retreat, a fucking magical place for residents who need extra care.

The fifty-seven acre facility is located outside Jackson, and there are manicured lawns and flowers everywhere you look, even though spring hasn't really sprung yet in Mississippi. It reminds me of somewhere a movie star might go if they needed a spa to recuperate at.

It's a damn far cry from the trailer park we grew up in.

Raven and I get a tour of the place, including the gym, indoor and outdoor pools, sauna, tennis courts, pottery studio, horse barn, and cinema. Hell, the place even has a bubble bar where you can make your own liquid with different colors then package it and give it away as gifts.

I want this to be where Raven will live, but I can't breathe every time I glance down at the dollar amount at the bottom of the paperwork Mrs. Watson, the admissions advisor, has given me.

She sits across from me in her office, the huge bay window behind her showcasing the horses that roam in the sprawling pasture.

Raven's disability compensation would only put a slight dent in the six-thousand-dollar monthly fee, but to even get on the list, I need fifty grand, which acts as a deposit to hold her spot and pays the first few months up front.

I feel like I might be sick.

I'm thankful Raven is sitting out in the waiting room.

"Is everything okay, Maverick?"

I look up into the kind face of Mrs. Watson. An older lady in her mid-fifties, I sense she can read right into my panic.

Once again, I'm regretting not going into the draft early, but it's too late now. Once you send your decision to the board, it's final, and you can't go back.

"Yes. Thank you for the tour and the information." I paste a smile on my face. There's no way in hell I can swing this place.

She nods, her hair carefully coiffed and pulled back at the nape of her neck. "In addition to your sister's fully furnished apartment, she'll have three nutritious meals served each day in our cafeteria, or she can opt to visit one of our onsite restaurants with friends or visitors. We have daily group activities and excursions to museums and other places of interest. Just last week we took a group to the Civil Rights Museum in Memphis." She laughs. "We even do Graceland once a year—talk about an interesting daytrip." She glances down at Raven's health history and shuffles through the papers. "I see she sustained a traumatic brain injury in a car accident a few years ago?"

I clear my throat. "Yes, she suffers from memory loss,

sporadic seizures—which can be avoided with medication—minor cognitive delays, and frequent headaches, which are easy to manage if she gets plenty of exercise. She was wheelchair bound for a year and still walks a bit off balance."

Her eyebrow rises. "You're very knowledgeable about your sister's health. That's impressive."

"I've done some research."

She nods. "We also provide counseling, as well as medical services and checkups. A full-time nurse is on her floor twenty-four hours a day."

Damn. That sounds like heaven. It would mean I could rest easy knowing she was being taken care of.

I sigh, getting to the crux of the matter. "I don't suppose you offer any financial aid options, do you? The cost is... steeper than I anticipated. I mean, I knew what to expect based on researching your facility online, but I wasn't sure if you had scholarships or some kind of assistance?"

I'm just hoping maybe I missed something.

She gives me a soft smile. "No, but I understand your reticence. It's quite the sticker shock."

"How soon could you get her in if I paid the deposit?"

She looks at her calendar and taps her pen on the desk. "If you pay in the next few weeks, I can pencil her in for the first of May."

Shit. That's just a few months away.

I'm meeting with Leslie in a few days, and I'm anxious to hear what his offer is and how soon I can fight.

Mrs. Watson pulls me back to the present. "I hate to be a pain, but would you mind signing an autograph for me?" She blushes. "My son will go nuts over it. Our family has followed your career since you were in high school."

"Of course." Feeling at a bit of a loss and still reeling from the idea of figuring this mess out, I sign the piece of paper she's slid over to me then hand it back to her.

"Great. Someday when you're in the NFL, this will be priceless—not that I'd ever sell it."

Right, but as a college student, I have zero money, and no one can give me money. It doesn't make any fucking sense.

I nod and stand. More than anything, I just want to get out of here, talk to Leslie about the fight, and figure this shit out. I shake her hand and mumble a thank you for the hasty meeting she agreed to then make my way out the door.

Raven walks as fast as she can when she sees me, her face still red from the brisk wind.

"See…the…apartments…again? Please?" She hates Dad's trailer, and I don't blame her. I can't keep running over there, trying to mesh two demanding worlds together into one.

I'm missing class today just to be at this meeting. God knows Dad isn't the one to come. When I showed up today to pick her up, he was still asleep. I was the one to make us breakfast, help her pick out her clothes, put a load of clothes in the wash, and usher her out the door.

I ruffle her hair, forcing lightness into my voice. She's sometimes quick to pick up on how I feel, and I like to think it's flashes of the old Raven, the one who made straight As in school and was a normal sixteen-year-old girl.

"We only get one tour. How about some ice cream at Buster's? You love their chocolate raspberry."

Her shoulders shift in a vulnerable way, as if she's preparing herself. "Pineview…won't…let…me…in?"

I laugh and hook our arms together as we walk down the hall and head toward the parking lot. "It just takes time to get you signed up, that's all."

She sighs. "Wish…I…could…snap…my…fingers… make…everything…how…it…used…to…be."

I swallow down the lump in my throat.

CHAPTER 15

DELANEY

He-Man: I'm sorry about the baseball party, Princess Leia. Forgive me?

Me: Why should I?

He-Man: Because we're friends.

Me: Are we?

He-Man: I hope so. I left a gift for you at the front desk of the library. Did you get it?

Me: Yes.

He-Man: Well? Do you like it?

Me: What's not to love about a full-size movie poster of *The Princess Bride*? Thank you.

He-Man: I may not be texting you as much. I've got some personal things going on, but that doesn't mean I'm not thinking about you.

Me: What's going on?

He-Man: Just…wait for me.

"Hey," comes a husky voice, and I flip around, dropping the book I was trying to shelve.

It's Maverick, and my eyes drink him in. His face appears tired, his expression somber as he studies me. It's been almost a week since the party, and things are weird. When he showed up for class on Monday, I'd switched seats on him, opting to sit in the front row. Maybe it was a test to see if he would follow me. He didn't. His eyes searched the room and found me, and though I saw disappointment there—or maybe relief—he took his usual seat in the back. On Wednesday, it was the same. He sat in the back, and I was down in front.

"We haven't talked since the party," Maverick says, bending down to pick up the book and hand it to me.

"Yeah," I mutter.

He tucks his hands in his pockets and leans against one of the racks, his gaze studying me intently. "Look, I'm sorry I didn't show up for salsa this week. Things are on hold with me right now. My dad is going through some things, and I'm spending a lot of time with my sister."

I give him a shrug, trying to be as nonchalant as I can when really I was devastated when he didn't show. I stood outside the door until the very last minute, hoping he'd appear. I didn't even have his phone number to text him.

"It's fine. You did miss some great plantains though." I've torn my eyes off him because he's too handsome, and I stare down at the cart of books I need to get shelved. "I need to get back to this…so if you don't mind, maybe we can chat later?"

He exhales and takes a step closer to me. "Delaney, I'm sorry…I just need to focus on football…" His voice trails off.

His words hurt, and it makes me angry that I've let my guard down and allowed him to get this close. "I'm sure you do have big things going on—football, and probably a different girl every night." It's not a fair assumption, but I can't stop the words from coming out.

He frowns. "It's not like that at all. I'm taking care of my sister, juggling classes and practice, and working through some other things."

"What things?"

He stiffens and shutters his face, not giving anything away, but this nerd girl can read him like a book: he's withdrawing. He doesn't want to share. He doesn't want *me*.

I let out a sigh. "Good luck with your life," I say as I grip the cart and push it down the aisle.

CHAPTER 16

MAVERICK

I'm at Carson's Gym, and I grunt out my displeasure when I take a direct hit to the face from my sparring partner. Rio, the guy Leslie has paired me up with, dances away from me, grinning around his big-ass mouthpiece. His hits are sneaky and he's got a mean left hook, but I'm bigger, faster, and light on my feet. Being in tune with my body and how it works is something I've always been good at. Boxing is second nature to me as well, something I took to in high school since my dad used to work here doing part-time janitorial duties.

My skill is the reason Leslie is interested in me—well, that and my name in football. He's standing down on the floor watching us, a cold look on his face, wearing a slick tailored suit. I've already met with him this week, and he's made it clear what he wants from me: a fight with another SEC football player. No rules, just me and another guy in a boxing ring. My gut churns at the prospect of putting everything on the line— my career, my whole fucking life.

A flash of white-blonde hair and a pink workout shirt coming out of one of the yoga classrooms gets my attention—

right as Rio plants a hit straight to my eye.

"Shit!" I bark and back away into the corner. At this rate, I'll really need to brush up on my skills if some chick in a tight top is all it takes to lose my focus.

I look back to the hallway, and my heart pounds as I realize it's Delaney—I know it from the Princess Leia buns she likes to wear. I haven't spoken to her since the library, and that was a few days ago.

She strides toward the gym foyer, and it looks as if she's been crying.

"Delaney! Wait!"

She pauses and looks over her shoulder at me, and once again I'm floored by how gorgeous she is. Wearing black yoga pants and a pink tank her breasts strain against, she is damn amazing, even with a tear-streaked face. Her cheeks are red, and she hurriedly wipes at them as I grab a towel and jump down from the boxing platform.

Her eyes widen as she watches me.

I call over my shoulder, telling Rio I'll catch him later, and I give Leslie a quick nod. I've gotten enough sparring in today and I'm done.

"Why are you crying?" I ask as I come to a stop in front of her, still breathing hard from the boxing.

"I'm not." She sniffs and turns her head away, giving me a view of her long neck, the soft lines of her jaw. My eyes greedily eat her up. I've missed her like crazy in class, and I'm a heel for not trying to explain things to her, but with the fight looming over me, I think it's best I keep my distance. Even so, that doesn't mean I haven't thought about her a hundred times.

"Why did you bolt out of the yoga class?" It's an activity I didn't even know she participated in.

She seems to gather herself slowly. "I know it seems silly, but Han Solo's been missing the past two days. I'm sure you don't get it…" Her voice trails off.

"What happened?" I take her arm and lead her over to a group of chairs in the foyer. Grabbing a box of Kleenex from the desk, I press them into her hand as she sits down.

She cleans up her face. "A couple of days ago, I let him out to stomp around like he likes to do, and he just never came back. I called for him and put out tuna fish on the back porch—nothing. It's not like him."

"Maybe he found a girlfriend?"

She shakes her head. "He's been spayed. What if he's in a ditch somewhere and I can't find him?"

"So why are you rushing out?" I glance back at the yoga room. "I didn't even know you took a class here."

"The campus rec center has the worst yoga classes. This one is much better, and I needed to get out of the house and let off some steam."

I nod.

"Anyway, my neighbor, Mrs. Wells, just called me. She thought she saw him on campus today near the fine arts building, and it's the first ray of hope I've had. I'm on my way there to look for him." She stands and holds out the box of tissues. "Thank you for asking." Her voice is shaky yet cool, and I sigh. I don't blame her for being standoffish with me.

"I'll go with you," I say, and she blinks.

"What? Why?"

I ignore that. I'm in take-charge mode, and when I see the coat she wears to class hanging near the door, I stride over to get it. Slipping it off the hook, I wrap her up in it and button it carefully.

She stands there watching me as I dash back to the boxing area and grab my gym bag.

I jog back to where she waits. "Now, let's go find Han Solo."

A smile briefly appears on her face and she gives me an odd look. "Are you sure? You're…" She clears her throat, her gaze lingering on my pecs. "You're half-naked and it's cold outside."

I grab my North Face off a hook and slip it over my bare chest. "I'm fine, Buttercup."

CHAPTER 17

DELANEY

Maverick ushers me out into the cold and straight to his truck, a Toyota that looks like it's seen better days. He opens the passenger door for me and gives me a hand up into the cab. He gets in on the other side, looks over at me, and squeezes my hand, surprising me. He's being so…sweet and helpful. "You okay?" he asks.

I nod. I'm worried about Han, but I'm also discombobulated by seeing Maverick at the gym, even though Skye casually mentioned this week that she heard a lot of the football players come to Carson's during the off season to take advantage of their programs.

Part of my reason for taking the yoga class here was hoping I'd run into him—so stupid, but I can't help myself.

"Why were you boxing?" I ask.

He shrugs. "My dad used to work there and was able to get me a few lessons when I was growing up. I'm pretty good at it."

"Is there anything you're not good at?"

"Nope." He sends me a grin and I try to reciprocate, but it

fails. Things are still strange between us. I sigh and look out the window.

We pull up to the fine arts building, and I'm out the door before he even gets us parked. My gaze scans the horizon, looking past trees and landscaping and buildings, trying to catch a flash of black and white fur. It feels futile, and I don't see anything that looks like him. At least it's the weekend and campus is dead, so there aren't a hundred bodies to look around.

"Han, where are you, little man?" calls Maverick as he takes the north side of the building and I take the south. Ten minutes of fruitless searching goes by as I make one more pass and then two across the quad in front of the surrounding buildings. Nothing is out here except for a few crazy squirrels and blackbirds.

I feel lost. Han #1 left, and now Han #2.

"Over here!" It's Maverick's voice, and I flip around to see that he's holding a squirming Han about fifty yards away. Pure joy fills me as I take off running toward them. Breathing heavily from my jog, I come to a stop, take the fighting Han, and pet him until he calms.

"Maverick! Oh my gosh, where did you find him?"

He shrugs. "Would you believe he was in the dumpster behind the building? He must have crawled in there for food and couldn't get out. I heard a tiny meow, opened it up, and there he was."

I rub his head the way he likes, and he nips at my hand then purrs.

Looking back up, I notice Maverick's jacket is torn and his

shorts look askew. My mouth opens. "You got in the dumpster?"

He grins. "Dumpster diver, at your service."

I throw my arms around him, somehow managing to not squish Han in the process. My lips graze his cheek for a second and he turns his head to meet them, but I pull away before that happens.

I react by looking down at my runaway cat. "What if no one had seen him all weekend? You probably saved one of his lives."

"Undoubtedly. I hope he's worth it."

I sigh. "He's all I have."

"Well, you have me now." He clears his throat. "He looks a bit frazzled. Let's get you both home."

We pull up at my house and it's nearly dark. Skye's car is gone, and I recall a text from her earlier saying she was staying at Tyler's place tonight.

I'm still holding Han in my arms and he's anxious to get down, so I get to the front door in a hurry. Maverick follows me, taking my keys from my bag and unlocking my door.

As soon as he gets it open, I plop the cat down and he takes off. "Now don't run away again," I scold him as he flounces toward the kitchen where his food and water are.

I gaze back at Maverick, who's watching me.

"What?"

He shrugs as he leans against the doorjamb and brushes

those gorgeous eyes over me. "Just like looking at you. I'm glad we found him."

"Me too," I sigh. "Well, thank you for taking me there and finding him."

Maverick starts, straightening up. "Oh, I just realized we didn't go get your car at the gym."

I shrug. "Don't worry about it. I'm not going anywhere else tonight, and Skye will be back tomorrow."

He chews on his lip. "Don't you have plans?"

"Nope. You?"

"No."

He watches me, studying me, and before I can stop myself, I blurt out, "Do you want to stay for dinner? I can cook for us —you know, as a thank you for helping me find Han. I don't think I would have been able to get him out of that dumpster even if I had heard him in there."

"I'd love that." An almost shy expression crosses his face. "I don't think anyone's ever cooked for me…you know, since my mom."

"Oh, that's too bad. Come in." I'm nervous, feeling him walking behind me as we enter the house and he checks out the place. It's nothing fancy, but it's all mine, built in the late eighties and only a block from campus.

Before I get to the kitchen, he grabs my hand, halting me. His expression is conflicted as he stares at me. "Hey, I'm sorry for being an ass lately, Delaney. I swear there's no one else. I'm just—"

"It's fine," I say. "I get it. You're busy."

It seems like he wants to say more, but he lets my hand go,

takes off his jacket, and tosses it across the back of the couch. I see his chest…his naked chest…and I swallow thickly.

Feeling breathless, I say, "Take a look in the fridge and decide what you'd like. I have a little bit of everything."

"You did mention nachos once," he says as he pulls out a pack of ground beef and holds it up.

I nod and he grins, making my face heat. "I did. Now move your ass so I can work my magic."

"Can I watch?" he says softly, crossing his arms over his chest as he leans against my fridge, perfectly showcasing his biceps and the ropes of muscle in his forearms.

I take a deep breath. "Sure. Hand me my apron, will you?" I say, turning on the stovetop and putting the beef in a pan. I tilt my head at the hooks along the back wall, and he strides over to pick up the black apron. He shakes it out and brings it over to me, and I expect him to hand it over, but he doesn't; instead, he slips the loop over my hair, his hands brushing lightly over my shoulders as he spins me around to tie the back. Blood pounds in my veins at the way he handles me, as if he's perfectly attuned to every nuance of my skin.

He spins me back around. "*May the Forks Be With You?*" He shakes his head as he reads the white words printed on the apron.

I ease away from him to stir the beef.

"You're such a nerd, Delaney."

"And your point is?"

His eyes light up. "I like it. I like a girl with a brain."

"Good. I like you too." I say the words lightly.

He's closer now, leaning against the fridge and watching

me as I work. His scent hits me—male with a hint of sweat—and I'm having a hard time keeping my eyes off his chest.

Just keep him at a distance, I tell myself, but the truth is I'm weak and tired of fighting this feeling. Maverick freaking Monroe is in my kitchen, without a shirt on, watching me cook like he wants to eat me instead of the food I'm preparing.

He tucks a strand of hair behind my ear, his hand drifting down my arm as he pulls away. "You're quite possibly the most beautiful girl I've ever met," he says softly as his thumb rubs at a spot on my shoulder, and I don't stop him, don't pull away. "You're nervous," he says, leaning in closer. "Are you trying not to sneeze?"

I clear my throat. "Actually, my sneezing seems to be better lately." It's true, and the more I'm around him, the sassier I'm becoming.

"Nice."

I fiddle with the pan. "Uh, do you want to find us a movie while I cook?" I gesture to the big screen in the den, which is easily visible from the kitchen with the open floor plan of the house.

"Sure. How about *The Princess Bride*?"

I drop the spatula in the pan and turn to look at him. A small grin curls his mouth.

"Why would you say that?"

His eyes lower. "I saw the poster you have up in the den."

Oh, right. I glance past him to the gift He-Man left for me at work. I already got it framed and up on the wall, and every time I look at it, I think about the mysterious man who gave it to me.

"It's one of my favorites," I say.

"Mine too."

I suck in a breath, my heart flying. I want to ask if he's He-Man…but I don't. "Yeah, sure, *The Princess Bride* sounds great. It's free on Netflix."

I work in the kitchen and listen to him as he fiddles with the remote, searching for the iconic classic. As I drain the meat and set it to the side, I work precisely and methodically, trying to keep my brain from piecing together what I know is true.

It *has* to be him. Too much has been similar, and I feel close to both of them.

I'm dicing tomatoes at the counter when he strides back into the kitchen, his piercing gaze sweeping over me. "Mind if I take a shower before we eat?"

"In my shower?"

"No, your neighbor's. Yes, yours."

"And you'll use my soap?" I picture him using my loofa too, rubbing it across that magnificent chest.

Another grin. "Is this a problem? Are you uptight about people using your stuff?"

"No." How do I explain that the image of him in my house with water spraying down on him…I shake myself. "Yes, of course you can shower. I-I just…what will you put on?"

He rakes a hand through his blond hair and scratches his jaw, which I notice has acquired a bit of a shadow. I wonder how it would feel between my…

"I can wear a towel," he says, a glint of glee in his eyes.

"No."

"One of your shirts?" His eyes brush over my chest.

"Too small."

He shrugs. "I can always just walk around naked." I throw a dishtowel at him and he catches it. "This?"

"No, goofball!" I huff out a laugh. He really is incorrigible. "Wait here, I think I have something."

I turn to head to my bedroom and hear him call out after me. "It better not be one of Alex's shirts."

I chuckle as I grab the garment I have in mind, a roomy shirt featuring a white cat wearing spectacles. I head back to the kitchen, thrust it into his hands, and push him toward the bathroom. He walks backward, letting me guide him, my hands on his forearms.

He's in the bathroom and I'm just standing here waiting for him to shut the door, but he doesn't right away. He's looking at me as if he wants to say something.

So do I.

I swallow, feeling breathless. "I…I have to ask you something."

"What?"

My chest catches as our eyes meet. I bite my lip. "Are you…He-Man?"

His chin goes up as his eyes lower to half-mast. "Damn, Buttercup, I've been waiting weeks for you to ask me that."

Maverick—*or should I say, He-Man*—is showering while I furiously set the table and finish making lemonade.

He's in my freaking shower…*naked*.

I check the clock on the wall. It seems like he's been in there forever, although in reality it's only been fifteen minutes. Feeling flustered by the images my mind is conjuring up, I march down the hall to knock on the door and let him know everything's done.

Just as I raise my hand, Han comes up behind me and puts his front paws on the bathroom door, which of course isn't shut all the way, so it opens. *Darn cat.*

I don't mean to spy on Maverick. Really it's just an accident that I peek through the crack in the door and see the mirror, which shows the glass shower enclosure…and his naked form. I swallow hard at his broad chest, his thick arms as he scrubs his hair, the drops of water as they run down his pecs to that deliciously tempting V, right down to his—

Our eyes meet in the mirror and I take a step back, out of sight.

Shit.

The water turns off.

I clear my throat. "Everything's ready," I say, projecting my voice.

The shower door opens and shuts. "Do you think dinner can wait?" he says.

I can't see his face, and it's killing me, so I step forward a little so we can talk. Before I realize it, my feet have taken me right into the bathroom, and it's not an accident. My body knows what it wants.

"Wait for what?" I say.

He's standing there in front of me, and I blink rapidly, my traitorous eyes tracking a wayward droplet of water as it skirts down his corded neck, past his shoulders, and to his legs.

"Buttercup, I think you know what."

The air is hot and humid, making my face damp as I stand within a few feet of him. My hands itch to touch him, to caress that utter perfection, that body that's been honed by years of hard work and training.

"Delaney," he says, and I hear the command in his tone, the sheer confidence that he knows I want him.

"You're naked," I say, averting my gaze and looking up at the ceiling.

"And you're not—why?"

I take a deep breath.

"Delaney." His tone is silky. "Look at me."

I do and my body shudders with built-up need, taking him in. *God*, I want to be naked. I want to throw myself all over him and satisfy this craving, but…

"I want you, Delaney, and it's killing me slowly."

I suck in a sharp breath as his hand moves to caress his hard cock. He's unapologetic and proud as he pumps from tip to root, his palms working over the velvety-looking skin of his hard, long member.

"He-Man has a big sword," I say breathlessly.

"Damn straight." He rolls his fingers over the mushroom-shaped head as he bites his lip, making *me* bite my lip. His breathing increases as his chest rises, and I'm filled with the need to be the one to make that noise come from him.

Desire swirls in his gaze. "This is all for you…*you*."

He releases his grip and I whimper, missing the sight of him pleasuring himself. He takes a step toward me and threads his hands through my hair, tugging at the pins that hold the buns together. With a touch so light it makes me shiver, he trails his fingers down the sides of my neck and onto my shoulders.

"You're wet," I say, watching the water drip down his chest.

"Are you?"

"Yes."

He murmurs his approval softly, and a thousand thoughts fly at me at once, telling me to stop, to not get this close to another athlete, but I'm past caring.

"This is crazy," I murmur.

"Crazy good," is his reply.

"It's probably a mistake," I add.

"Best fucking mistake ever," he says before taking my mouth, his full and sensuous lips sliding over mine, parting them until I sink into him and revel in the sensation of him against me.

Strong hands cup my face as his tongue tangles with mine, and I put my hands on top of his then whimper with need.

"Delaney," he whispers in my ear as his mouth explores the tender curve of my neck and the hollow of my throat. His teeth nip at my skin, and I groan out his name.

With a deftness that doesn't surprise me, he has me out of my pink workout top and sports bra. He backs me up against the wall and kisses me, sighing into my mouth as my hands snake around his shoulders and cling to him. His cock is pinned between us, pressing into me, and I swivel my hips against it.

His hand skates across my breast teasingly and his mouth

follows, capturing my nipple and making me moan.

Is it possible to orgasm with just this?

Why am I surprised? It's *him*.

His hand curls around my ass and my leg hooks around his hip, needing friction. With a groan, he pushes my yoga pants down to my feet, puts my leg back around his hips, and slides his fingers underneath my panties. I'm thankful I put on the pink lace ones this morning, but those thoughts vanish as his fingers brush back and forth, teasing my clit and the entrance to my core. He fingers me slow and then fast, his lips sucking my collarbone as I toss my head back and take in much-needed air. The scent of him fresh from the shower, the wetness of his skin, the sheer beauty of him—it all overwhelms me.

My pelvis moves with him as my spine tingles, the energy building and heating my insides. I'm putty in his hands as he touches me, his forehead pressing against mine.

"You're dripping for me," he says, and I moan. I can't do anything else but be at his mercy as he plays me. Our breaths mingle together and when our eyes meet, I combust.

Fireworks go off as I come, my body vibrating against his hand, my walls reverberating with bliss. I place both hands on his shoulders to hang on, the aftershocks of the quake keeping my body undulating against him. He watches intently, that piercing gaze of his so open and honest and needy that I reach up and kiss him.

"That was…" I don't know what to say. Amazing seems so cliché; so does awesome.

He seems to know I have no words, looking as bemused as I am by our explosive chemistry. "I didn't plan on this. I was just taking a shower and I saw you..." He swallows, his eyes searching my face. His arms curl around my waist. "Do you want more?"

I feel his cock brushing against my panties, which are now back in place. All it would take is for him to push that fabric aside and slide into me.

"I'll be your scabbard," I murmur, and he flashes me a grin then swoops me up in his arms.

"You're a nut," he says as I point him to my bedroom amid giggles.

He's not even winded by carrying me, and I sink into his skin, wanting to bury myself in him.

He laughs as he sets me on my bed and scoots me over until we're under my covers, face-to-face.

"You okay?" he asks.

I pause, my brain spinning. I've had a moment to think between here and the bathroom, and I'm not sure.

It's like he reads my mind. "I'm not him, Delaney. I'm never going to cheat on you."

I swallow. "So this isn't just a spur-of-the-moment hook-up?"

His hand on my waist tugs me closer. "It's going to take a million hook-ups to get you out of my head."

My body curls into his as he pulls me against his chest and kisses me again, harder this time.

He works his way down my body at a leisurely pace, his lips toying with my nipples, plucking at them with his teeth.

I'm moaning as he slides farther down, his mouth finding secret places on my skin, the bend of my knee, the inside of my thigh. When his tongue slides across my clit, my lower body bows up and clenches, on the verge once again.

His hand pushes my chest down, holding me firmly in place as he works me over with the dance of his mouth. He devours me, giving me everything and not holding back. I'm panting when he finally comes up for air, my body trembling, ready to explode.

"Maverick." I taste his name on my lips, and it's so good. My hands tug him up to me, caressing his chest and hips, learning his skin. We kiss deeply, and the heat between us is the hottest I've ever been for another person in my life. His cock begs for me to take it in my hands, and I do, running my fingers over his length, lightly teasing the tip.

"Do you have condoms?" he asks between kisses.

I nod toward the nightstand. He reaches over, opens the drawer, and grabs one. I'm impatient, stroking him with my palms as he tears it with his teeth and slides it on.

He positions himself and enters me slowly, easing his thickness inside my entrance and then darting out, making me moan.

"More," I tell him.

He pumps inside, soft and slow and barely there, making me crazy.

"Please," I beg.

He bends his forehead to mine and kisses me as he adjusts my hips for a better angle, and then he slides all the way in, to the hilt, his girth filling me up tight as he moves inside me. With him on his knees, he takes me, hard and fast, his breath coming in pants as he works above me.

"All mine, Delaney." His words are broken up, and I can tell he's into this. There's an intensity to him, and he's staring at me like he'll never let me go.

Arching his back, his fingers rub at my pussy, playing me in a synchronized rhythm with his thrusts. I come apart.

He watches me with a heavy-lidded gaze, his eyes eating up every detail of my orgasm. "That's what I was waiting for, Buttercup."

With a shout, he comes after me, his body tightening and straining as his cock hardens inside me, his body pumping out every last bit of sensation.

"Damn," he says after a few moments of lying on top of me. His chest is heaving as he slides out and lies down next to me.

"What?" I ask.

"That was…that was…"

"The best?" I ask.

He grins. "I know it was for you."

I smack him with a pillow and he laughs, pulling me into his arms for an embrace.

Later, we're cuddling and talking in the dark.

"I can't believe you're He-Man," I say, gazing up at him. "I'm still processing."

He grins down at me. "I know. I was going to tell you at the party, but then the other stuff happened with Alex." He plays with a strand of my hair. "Ryker was the one who first texted you that night."

"Did he know who I was?"

"He just knew I'd torn a girl's phone number off of the salsa sign you'd put up. I didn't tell him *who* it was because I knew he'd be worried about the whole Alex thing. You should have seen his face when I told him it was Delaney Shaw. He freaked out."

"Speaking of Alex…what's going to happen now?"

He looks over at me. "Alex has nothing to do with us," he sighs. "Hell, just you saying his name pisses me off."

Oh. I bite my lip. "I mean, I know you have a lot going on, and I don't want to mess up your game—or his."

But isn't this feeling worth it? I don't say that, but I'm thinking it. My feelings for Maverick have merged with those I've developed through the texts with He-Man, and I'm in deep even though I know it's dangerous to my heart.

"Football doesn't start until this fall. He's got time to get used to us."

Us?

I smile and he leans in to kiss me. "Ready for round three?"

I laugh. "You think you're up for it?"

"I'm up for anything with you."

My heart swells.

The voice of Taylor Swift singing "Shake it Off" comes from another room. It sounds like a ringtone, but it's not mine.

He heaves out a sigh and scrubs at his chiseled face. "Dammit."

"Is that your ringtone?"

"Yeah, my sister's. I need to go. I forgot I was supposed to check in on her tonight."

"Oh...okay."

He stands up, his head seemingly already somewhere else, and I do as well, grabbing a robe from the back of the bedroom door to slip on. He's already dashed to the bathroom, grabbed his gym shorts, and put them on.

"I wish I didn't have to rush off, but I'm staying there tonight because my dad's helping a buddy out at his garage." He grimaces. "It's extra cash for them, so..."

I tighten my belt, following him out into the hall. "You do that a lot when he's gone?"

He shrugs. "Sometimes on the weekends. Raven doesn't need to be alone."

How does he have a life?

"How do you do that between school and football?"

"Most days I'm barely hanging on." A gruff laugh comes out of him as he quickly checks his appearance in the hall mirror, arranging his hair. "But really, her living with my dad didn't start until after football season. If this had happened during the season, I'd have been screwed." He rubs at the scruff on his jaw.

"Where was she before your dad's?"

His teeth clamp together, and I know I've hit a nerve. "She was at a state-funded group facility paid for by insurance, but we weren't happy with it. She had bruises and no one could explain them."

I inhale. "That's terrible. What happened when you asked?"

"Nothing. It's a shitty place and I couldn't leave her there, so we put her with my dad temporarily—but that comes with its own problems."

Wow. It's a lot to take in.

He must read my face. "Don't worry about me. I can handle it."

I clear my throat. "Do you want me to come with you? I mean, I don't mind hanging out with you guys. We can watch TV or play a game or something?"

He rubs his hand across his lips and considers me, a frown twisting his face as he considers what to say.

"Maybe next time." He kisses me on the lips, cupping my cheek. "I'll text you, okay?"

I nod.

But…

I know he's not telling me everything.

There's a cagey look on his face, a wary expression that pricks at me.

Stop worrying, Delaney.

I want to, but now that the fun is over, my head is reminding me to guard my heart.

If you're going to do this with him, be careful.

I head into the kitchen to pack up the food. "Okay, at least take this with you. I'm sure you guys need dinner." I busy myself getting out containers to put at least half the nachos in, leaving some out for me.

"Delaney…" His voice is soft as he looks around at the preparation I did while he was showering. I chopped tomatoes and lettuce and got cheese and guacamole out of the fridge. I even put out real plates when I normally only use paper. I blush. "I didn't do anything but make nachos."

"You're incredible." He takes the containers of food I hand him, gives me one last look, and then he's out of the kitchen and out my door.

I watch him go, hoping like hell I'm not going to get hurt.

CHAPTER 18

DELANEY

I'm ready for class on Monday at least an hour before it starts. Part of it is that I didn't sleep well over the weekend, thinking about Maverick and Raven and how much pressure that must be when he's so young and has such a big future ahead of him.

Since I haven't seen him since Saturday, I take extra care with my hair, blowing it out and straightening it until it's a thick blonde curtain. Last night, I carefully scoured my wardrobe and came up with a tight-fighting lilac sweater and a pair of smoke-gray skinny jeans that curve over my bum. Now, with a careful hand, I apply extra dark red lipstick.

I saunter out to grab a cup of coffee and find Skye sitting at one of the barstools at the island, her head bent as she inhales her early morning brew.

"What's up, girlie," I call out, and she just grunts. She isn't a morning person like I am. "I made some chocolate chip cookies this weekend if you want some," I tell her as I breeze by to grab a mug from the cabinet. "Nana's recipe."

She gives me a little mumble.

I pour my coffee and toss in a healthy amount of French vanilla creamer from the fridge. "They are your favorite, right?"

She nods, her hands gripping her cup as she lifts it up for a long swig.

"Skye? Are you okay?"

She shakes her head. "Not really."

I sigh. I should have known something was up when she came in last night and didn't even pop her head in to say good-night. Normally she'd check in with me on a Sunday just so we could recap the weekend.

"Did you and Tyler fight?"

She raises her head, and I see dark circles under her eyes from lack of sleep. She grimaces. "I know, I look like hell. I slept horribly—I'm surprised I didn't keep you up with my tossing and turning."

I was doing my own tossing around in bed.

"What did Tyler do?" I say.

She grunts out a laugh. "Funny how you knew this was about him," she sighs. "We were at the baseball house watching a movie with a bunch of people and he just started…being a dick and ordering me around, like he expects me to be his maid or something. He asked me to clean his room and I told him to fuck off. Then I go to the bathroom and when I come back, there's some stupid girl in his lap."

My stomach drops. *What a douchebag!*

She bites her lip. "So I get pissed and we have words then he kicks me out of the house and tells me not to come back until I'm *ready to apologize*." She uses air quotes.

"I'm so sorry." I always knew he was a jerk, but of course, I don't say that.

A tear makes its way down her face and immediately I'm next to her with my arms around her shoulders as she leans into me. "Hey, don't cry."

Her hands tighten around her coffee mug. "Ugh. I can't believe I've spent the past few months dating him."

I rub her back. "You know what? Let's plan our spring break trip tonight. Going to the beach always makes you feel better. We'll lay out in the sun and forget all about our ex-boyfriends."

She nods, wiping at her face. "How was your weekend?"

I almost tell her about Maverick, but then decide to wait. "It was great." I hand her the container of cookies and pop the top, letting the scent of sugar and chocolate waft around us.

She lets out a long sigh. "God, those smell amazing."

"Five hundred calories each, but who the hell cares?"

She takes one and smiles.

Later, I arrive at class and take my seat in the back of the auditorium. When our professor arrives and Maverick still hasn't shown up, I'm nervous. The teacher is adamant about attendance, and there's no excuse for missing a test unless you're practically hospitalized. Then again, he is an athlete, and I know from experience they get away with missing class all the time. Still, that isn't really Maverick's style. The man has a brain to go along with all that brawn.

So, where is he?

I feel odd as I look through the history of the text conversations with He-Man. I have a different perspective now that I know it was Maverick. It was Maverick who rescued me from my blind date, showed up at the grocery store, and dared me to say I was a badass in the library. I change his name in my phone to Mav-Man and send him a text.

Where are you? We have a test today.

Not coming today. I'll explain later.

The professor approaches me to give me a stack of papers that are part of the test, and I slide my phone into my bag after switching it to silent.

Whatever he's doing, I hope all is well.

CHAPTER 19

MAVERICK

"There must be at least three hundred people packed in this ballroom," Ryker mutters as he stands next to me on Monday afternoon, surveying the milling crowd. "And they're all rich assholes."

I tighten the fingerless leather gloves on my hands and focus on taking deep breaths. Instead of being at Waylon today, we both skipped class to drive to Tunica, Mississippi, for the fight. We're standing in the corner of a ring underneath a glittering chandelier inside a riverboat casino owned by Leslie.

Standing in my corner as we wait, Ryker grimaces. "This place reeks of cigarette smoke. God, I hate casinos."

I force a laugh, shaking off my nerves as I do a few air punches and bounce around on my feet. "Isn't this the first time you've been to one?"

He shrugs. "Still don't like them. This place is trouble."

Hell yeah it is, yet here we are.

I look around the room, taking in the high-dollar crowd sporting tailored suits and tailored gowns. Just to get in the door, the crowd had to get Leslie's personal approval as well as put up several grand. The kicker is I have to *win* to get the fifty grand I negotiated.

My stomach feels like it's filled with lead, and I'm doing my damnedest to keep my eyes averted from the stares of the women and men who have their eyes on me as they sip from champagne flutes.

"Don't look at them," Ryker says firmly. His mouth is a thin straight line, and his face is harder than I've ever seen it. He hates that I've made this decision and he doesn't approve, but he's the kind of friend who's not going to leave my side.

"I just want it over with."

He swivels his head as the competition stalks into the ballroom from a side door. It's a showoff of an entrance by a monster of a man. He's around my age, flanked by two girls in low-cut dresses. He stops in the middle of the aisle, letting the spotlight dance over his broad chest as he puffs up and does a strut up to the ring.

He's massive, at least a couple of inches taller than me, which puts him around six-six. Swirls of brightly colored tattoos cover nearly every inch of his thickly muscled skin. Appearing to be of Polynesian descent with a wide chiseled face and a braid of long hair, he smirks at the crowd, shaking hands with some of the attendees.

I hear a sharp inhalation from Ryker. "Is that Kai Willis, the linebacker from Ole Miss? Goddamn, he's huge."

I exhale, the lead in my stomach getting heavier. "Shit." Ole Miss is our biggest rival in the SEC and "Killer" Kai is their star linebacker, so it makes sense that Leslie would want us to fight.

Ryker shakes his head and whistles as his gaze sweeps over the crowd. "What a bunch of sick bastards."

I nod. "People get off on this. They like seeing blood."

That hard look settles back on his face as he focuses on me. "Yeah, but you're jeopardizing everything."

Maybe.

He grimaces. "And why are there no cell phones? Why did we have to get patted down before we entered the room?"

"Leslie's protecting his fighters. He assured me this won't get out to the press."

He exhales. "The entire state of Mississippi will tear him apart piece by piece if he screws with their hometown Magnolia boy."

A muscle flexes in my jaw. Yeah, I'm a hometown boy with nothing but the clothes on my back.

Kai's face is impassive as he studies me from across the ring. Big, mean, and full of vitriol, he's one of the most formidable offensive players in the country. He stalks over to us, his eyes low as they take in every facet of my physique.

He stops in front of me and just stands there, a curl to his lip. "Never seen you without all the padding," he tells me, a sly tone to his voice. "Not impressed."

I shrug. "Impressive is when I kick your ass back to Oxford."

He tosses his head back and lets loose with a booming laugh before quickly sobering and leveling me with a cold stare. "You're going back to Waylon in a body bag. I've been doing this a long time, and you're the perfect little pretty boy for me to toss around today." He flexes his arms, bending his elbows and flexing his muscles in a strong man-style showoff as he does a little pirouette in front of me. "You can't beat this, pretty boy. I'm gonna kill you." There's a wild glint to his eyes, and part of me believes he wants to.

I force a shrug, playing it cool. He's trying to rile me up, and I can't let him. "We beat you on the field this year, Kai, and I'm going to beat you in that ring." I tap my head. "See, you may have those big steroid muscles going on, but I'm smarter."

He sneers at me as he gets up in my face. Someone from the crowd gasps as we catch the attention of the betters.

I arch a brow, not flinching. "Scary. Now fuck off and wait for the bell to ring."

He barks out that bellowing laugh, flips around, and stomps away.

I study him, trying to figure out what his strengths and weaknesses are. He has me on size, but that could be an advantage if I'm faster.

I stretch out and begin my routine of small punches. I flick my eyes over to Ryker, who has a deep scowl on his face. "I got this, Mama Ryker. Just be here when I'm done."

He lets out a long exhalation as he studies me, his hand sliding over his jaw. "Always, man. I'm not going anywhere until this shit is done."

Kai is killing me.

I take a punch straight to the jaw and it sends me reeling. I hit the ground on my ass and blink up at the chandelier, the bright lights competing with the birds that are flying around my head.

Get up, I hear Ryker say.

I look over at him with one eye because the other is completely shut from a hit I took in the last round. Blood runs down and clouds my vision as I swipe at it.

Kai is standing over me and delivers a kick straight to my ribcage.

I choke out a gasp and focus. *Fuck.* I'm drifting, my mind wandering because I've been hit one too many times.

I scramble up and dart away from Kai's massive legs to rest against the ropes. He approaches with his gloves up, his mouthpiece filled with saliva mixed with blood. I've gotten in a couple of good hits to his wide face, but it's like banging my hand against concrete.

His fist connects with my hip and I stumble back again.

Ryker is yelling at me from the sidelines, but I can't hear what he's saying. The crowd cheers and shakes their fists, some for me and some for Kai. Loud rock music blares from the speakers, and all the lights are out except for the spotlight that's narrowed in on the ring.

Panting through the mouthpiece, I bounce around on the ropes, moving away from Kai. *God dammit.* I need a fucking minute to get myself together.

Raven.

Pineview.

Fifty thousand dollars.

I shake myself off and roll my neck, barely pausing before I rush at him, my first strike clipping his shoulder, not the chest like I wanted, but the hit has enough force that he stumbles a bit. He barrels back at me, his legs maneuvering a roundhouse kick that plants right into my side.

He bounces away. "Second-degree black belt, asshole. Anything goes in this fight—didn't you know that?"

I narrow my good eye at him, my fists curling. "Mississippi boys learn how to fight for real in their fucking sleep. Karate isn't going to help you."

I wipe sweat out of my eyes, square off again, and eye him, looking for chinks in his armor. He's proficient in MMA, but boxing is where my strengths lie, and that's what I focus on.

Bobbing around him, my fists are up as I dart sideways, moving in and out, teasing him then popping just out of reach. I land a small right uppercut to his jaw, and he comes right back at me with a quick two-handed jab. I block it with my forearms and retaliate with an uppercut to his gut.

Whoosh. He grunts and bends over to catch his breath but pops right back up.

He maneuvers behind me, and this time I'm ready before he kicks, managing to block him with a punch to his thigh.

He growls out a curse and backs up, a slight limp to his normal swagger, and my fist aches inside the glove—it was a good solid blow.

He shifts around, eyeing me. He thinks I should be down by now.

I force a grin, knowing I probably look maniacal.

He comes at me again, his swipe a hair too wide, and I duck. He breathes heavily as he chases after me.

"Stop playing and take him down!" one of the men from Kai's corner calls out.

"Go back to Ole Miss!" Ryker yells back.

Kai runs at me head down, in football mode, and I anchor myself, waiting. He gets a second from knocking me on my ass, I sidestep like a good boxer, and he misses completely, lurching into the ropes.

I rush at him, landing a punch to his lower back.

Score.

Using my shoulder, I pop him in the chest and send him reeling.

Stay down, asshole, my face is telling him.

But he gets back up, his eyes glazed.

"You done?" I pant.

"Pussy," he calls at me as he slings blood out of his face.

"Your funeral," I say and raise my fists up.

My words spur him into action and he rushes at me again. He lands a strike to my spleen, and I thrash away to get my breath back. *Fuck.*

"Killer! Killer! Killer!" some of the Ole Miss fans chant.

It's like he brought his own cheering section.

I spare a glance at Ryker, and he screams out that there's a minute left in the round.

I'm not sure I can last sixty more seconds without a breather.

Kai advances again, on the offense, and I skirt around him, my feet skipping on purpose. If I can't take him down, maybe I can distract him. I make my way over to the crowd of people who've congregated in Kai's corner, cross my left arm into my inner right elbow, and pull it up—the universal sign for *fuck you*. The crowd roars its approval while Kai's fans shake their fists at me. I prance off, forcing my body to move like it isn't screaming in pain.

He runs at me, more sluggish than before, and I square off and wait. I suspect he's going to throw more fancy karate moves at me, and he does, his legs kicking at me as his fist aims for my face. I turn my body sideways and he misses, the inertia of his movement making him stumble. Before he recovers, I hit him in the head and he pops back with a dazed expression.

Down he goes like a rock off the side of a cliff.

"Hell yeah!" Ryker screams from the side, and I look around for Leslie, who motions for the ref standing off to the side. He jumps in and checks on Kai, who hasn't even twitched. His chest is rising and falling so at least I know he's breathing—I don't want anything serious to be wrong with him.

"Winner!" the ref yells as he holds up my hand.

I take a walk around the ring, eyeing the people in the audience. Some are cheering—*thank you, fellow Waylon fans*—while some are surly and sneer at me. *Whatever.*

It's fucking over.

CHAPTER 20

DELANEY

Mav-Man: I miss you.
Me: Me too. Will I see you today?
Mav-Man: No. I'll see you soon, Buttercup. Just…be patient and wait for me.

"This donut is the best thing I've ever put in my mouth," I murmur in reverence as Skye and I sit inside the pastry shop at the student center. The books for our next class are piled on the table where we've been studying. A popular hangout, the place is packed with students milling around before class on this Tuesday morning.

She picks at her donut, a sparkly thing with white icing and purple glitter, as she watches Tyler. Sitting at a table a few feet from us with several baseball players, Bobby Gene included—someone who is obviously too nice for Tyler—he's been glaring at us since they came in. He also sent Skye a few nasty texts over the past two days. So far, she hasn't responded, and I approve of her decision to dump him and move on.

"He's leaving," I tell her, watching as he picks up his trash and throws it away. "And, dammit, the douche is coming over here."

"Ugh." Skye wipes her fingers on a napkin, her body stiffening.

"You got this, girlie. Be polite, but don't let him talk down to you," I tell her.

He arrives at our table, tall and looming over us with a glower on his face. He brushes his eyes over me dismissively then turns to Skye, a curl to his lip. "You haven't replied to my texts. Still pissed at me, I suppose?"

"You told me not to come back until I'm ready to apologize." Her face reddens as if remembering how he kicked her out of the frat house. "I'm not going to apologize—ever."

His lips flatten, his face hardening.

"Bye, Tyler," I say, waving at him. "We're trying to eat here—alone."

He spears me with a glare. "You stay out of this."

"Just leave…please," Skye tells him, her eyes brighter than normal.

He utters a slur—*the dreaded C-word*—making her pale, and my hands clench as several heads turn in our direction. His comment was loud and clear, and now we're the center of attention inside the shop.

Skye is biting her lip and I'm about to stand up and go off on him when suddenly Alex is standing there, a scowl on his face as he looks at Tyler. "What's going on?"

"He's calling Skye names and being a dickhead," I say.

"Dude, back off," Alex tells him. "They're girls—what's wrong with you?"

Tyler huffs as he takes in Alex's tight face, probably debating whether or not it's worth it to start something. He hitches his backpack up on his shoulder and sends a heated glance at Skye. "Whatever. This is the end of us, bitch. I hope you're happy."

We watch as he stalks off, and I heave out a sigh of relief.

My eyes go back to Alex. I'm still a little ticked at him for the whole baseball episode, but I'm thankful he came over.

"Thanks," Skye says to him as she chews on her lip. "I-I didn't know what to say." She holds up her half-eaten donut. "Want the rest of this as a thank you?"

"Uh, I already have one." He holds up a to-go bag. "I was just walking past when I heard what he said to you. I couldn't let him get away with it." He grimaces and shuffles his feet, looking awkward.

I clear my throat. "He and Skye broke up over the weekend."

He nods, sending Skye a rueful look. "I see. Been there." His eyes are regretful as they find mine. "Uh, since I'm here and you're here…I want you to know I'm sorry about the baseball party. I shouldn't have jumped in between you and Maverick like that."

I blink.

He sighs, his face solemn as he rubs the back of his neck. "I've been thinking about it—about everything, and I hope you can forgive me someday for cheating on you."

Oh.

He takes a deep breath. "And I'm not going to bother you anymore—or Maverick. I won't stand in his way."

This is good...well, except that I haven't even seen Maverick since we were together. Sure, he's texted me, but he has yet to tell me why he missed class.

Alex exhales. "Do you think you can ever forgive me?"

I take in his slouched shoulders, the contrite expression on his face as he watches me anxiously.

"Yes," I tell him sincerely as something clicks in my heart, and it just feels right. I don't want him to be unhappy. We had some great times together, and most of all, we were always friends. I hold my hand out. "Friends," I say with a little smile.

He takes it and we shake.

The next morning before class, I'm standing outside Maverick's dorm room to check on him. I already sent him a text asking if he's going to show up, but he hasn't responded. Part of me is worried, and a bad feeling looms over me, one I won't be able to shake until I see him.

I rap out a quick knock and hear scuffling from inside the apartment-style residence.

"Who is it?" comes a muffled voice.

"Delaney Shaw."

The door flies open and I blink at the image in front of me.

With his wavy brown hair, Ryker has been caught unaware if his leopard print bikini underwear is anything to go by.

I clear my throat. *Good lord.* He's got hair everywhere, his chest a gold mine of curls.

He leans against the doorjamb and rubs the scruff on his

face, completely unconcerned that he's only wearing a banana hammock.

"Morning, Ryker."

He throws a look over his shoulder before coming back to face me. "Mav's asleep."

"He isn't going to class?"

"Uh—" He flounders, clearly not wanting me to come inside.

But I'm determined.

"Do you have any coffee made?" I ask sweetly.

"Why?"

I smile and hold up my paper bag of goodies. "Because coffee would go great with these chocolate muffins I made."

He sucks in a long breath as I open the bag and show him the contents, the appetizing scent of sugar and butter wafting up out of the bag. Ryker grins at me. "He said you like to cook, and I can't resist home-cooked food. Come on in."

I step inside, heading straight to the little kitchenette. Like Alex's dorm suite, the space has a small kitchen, a den, bedrooms off to the right, and a bathroom to the left.

Ryker sinks his teeth into a muffin as I dig around in the pantry to find what I need to make coffee.

"Goddamn, you're amazing," he murmurs as he reaches for a second muffin. "If Maverick isn't into you, how about we spend a little time alone?" He waggles his brows at me, clearly joking, making me shake my head.

"Maverick *is* into her," comes a gruff voice from behind me as two strong arms wrap around me and a nose finds my neck and inhales. "Damn, I've missed you."

My body melts into his. *God...yes.* This is what I need.

Ryker rolls his eyes at us. "Okay, you two, keep it PG."

Feeling glad that he's here and okay, I turn around only to have my heart fall.

He stands there in bare feet, navy flannel pajama pants, and a white t-shirt with one eye swollen shut and his left cheek colored yellow and purple from a bruise. His arms are painted with bruises too, most of them on his biceps.

For a moment, I can't breathe. I feel sick. Swallowing down my panic, I say, "What happened to your face? Are you okay?" My hands flutter around him.

He shakes his head. "Nothing you need to worry about. It's all over now."

What? Nothing to worry about? Is he crazy?

"Who did this to you?" I'm assuming it was a fight.

His face tightens, his gaze not meeting mine. "I got in a fight with someone at the bar when I went to pick up my dad this weekend."

My brow furrows, trying to imagine it. "That's horrible."

Ryker seems displeased with Maverick's response and lets out a sigh. Maverick scowls back at him, his jaw clenching.

I look from one to the other. "What on earth is going on? Is there something you're not telling me?"

Maverick doesn't respond, just strides over to the coffee. I watch as he lifts his arm to get a cup from the cabinet, the movement slow and careful.

My frustration with the lack of details grows. "This is why you weren't in class?"

Ryker snatches another chocolate muffin from the container and makes his way around us. "Looks like you two need to talk, and I need to put some clothes on." He walks by, giving me an apologetic look. "Good luck," and then he's out of the room and shutting his bedroom door.

"What the hell is going on here?" I ask Maverick as he stirs in creamer and settles back against the counter to sip his coffee.

"Just got in a tussle. It's not anything I want you to worry about."

"I am worried."

"Why?" Those intense blue eyes study me.

"Because you look terrible and I'm afraid you're hurt."

"Why?" He takes a long drag from his mug.

I lift my hands in exasperation. "Because I like you and I don't want bad things to happen to you."

He exhales loudly as he sets down his coffee, the movement making him wince. Because he's an alpha male, he's probably holding back some of his discomfort, so I know he's in a lot of pain. My eyes roam over him, taking in the way he gingerly moves forward to retrieve one of the muffins and sinks his teeth into it.

My lips compress. "Were the police involved? Because you need to file charges against the person who did this to you."

"No." Silence fills the room, and I stand here, not feeling entirely welcome. I'm disappointed and angry he isn't being more forthcoming.

Fine. I inhale sharply and snap up my backpack, which I set on the floor next to the table when I came in.

I'm at the door when I hear his voice.

"Delaney, please…don't go."

I freeze, my chest rising at his plea. His tone is soft, with an undercurrent of vulnerability that gives me pause.

I hear scuffling and turn around to watch him walk toward me. His steps are slow, his jaw clenched, his chest barely moving as if he's restraining even his own breaths.

"Dammit, you're really hurt," I say, biting my lip as I drop my backpack and walk over to him.

"I don't want you to go." He swallows and stares down at his feet.

"Let me see everything," I say, pulling up his loose shirt and gasping as I see the bruises on his ribs. A long one stretches down his right side, ending just above his hip. I clench my jaw and gaze up at him as tears prick at my eyes. This wasn't just a regular good-ol'-boys tussle.

"Maverick? This is…this is…"

"I'm okay," he says soothingly, cupping my cheek. "Get that worried expression off your face. I've been checked out by a friend, got some X-rays, and nothing's broken or fractured. I'll be fine, and I'll be back at practice in a week. Coach Al and my professors think I had a fender bender."

I lace my fingers with his and squeeze. "You're scaring me. Are you going to tell me what happened?"

His forehead presses against mine. "Just trust me, okay? Are you in a hurry to get to class?"

I shake my head as his eyes hold mine.

He kisses me lightly on the lips. "Good. Come back to bed with me."

My body gets hot at the words.

"You can't have sex like this…can you?"

He huffs out a laugh, and a smile—the first one I've seen today—flashes across his face. "I can have sex even if I'm half-dead, but right now, I just want to hold you."

There's a neediness in his gaze, and it makes me protective of him.

He tugs me toward a door and I follow him as we enter his bedroom. The bed is a full with a plaid duvet, and there's a dresser against the wall. His laptop and books are scattered across the foot of the bed, and he grunts as he moves them to a chair next to the door. I'm itching to offer to help, but I can sense he doesn't want me to.

I have a design class at noon, but I know I'm not going to make it, especially when he slowly pulls his shirt off by tugging at it from the neck. I get an unobstructed view of his magnificent chest as it slips over his hair then gets tossed to the floor. Next are his flannel pants. He kicks them off and stands there proudly, bruises and all, and I probably look like I need a fan in my face to cool me down.

"Want me to open a window, Buttercup?"

I smirk.

He hits me with those piercing eyes. "Take your clothes off. I want your skin against mine." There's that need in his tone again.

I take my coat off and toss it on the chair. My shirt and jeans are next, until I'm standing in my black lace demi-bra and matching panties.

A long sigh slips through his lips as his eyes caress me. "Damn."

Moving tentatively, he gets in the bed, lies back on the

pillows, and pats the spot next to him, a searching expression on his face. "It's like I wished you were here, Delaney, and you appeared. Thank you for checking on me."

I swallow. Part of me wants to get to the bottom of what happened, but for now, it doesn't feel right. I crawl in beside him and lie down, our bodies touching lightly; I don't want to hurt him. His arms curl around me, and everything else fades away.

Whatever's going on with him, I'll figure it out later.

CHAPTER 21

MAVERICK

Delaney taps her chin, thinking. "My biggest TV-slash-movie pet peeve is that Han Solo and Princess Leia never got enough on-screen kissing time." She looks over at me. "What's yours?"

I grin at her. It's been over a week since the fight, and most of the bruises on my face have faded to a light blue. I've been wearing sunglasses and a ball cap everywhere, and my story of a minor car accident seems to be accepted. I hate lying to everyone, but it's necessary.

We're sitting inside Buffalo Bills after salsa lessons, and Delaney's on a quest to figure out the real Maverick. I get the feeling once she becomes interested in something, she's devoted to it with a one-track mind. I can relate because I'm the same with football.

She's wearing a flowing red skirt and a pale blue sweater with a deep V-neck that clings to every curve. I'm trying not to stare at her full breasts, but I'm a Neanderthal and can't help it.

She waves a hand in front of my face. "Hello, is anyone listening?"

"Right. Back to your twenty questions," I say teasingly.

She stabs one of the fries on her plate. "If you didn't want to play, you should have just said so. I just thought it would be a good way to get to know each other."

I grin. "I can think of a few other ways."

She blushes furiously.

We've shared a lot since she came to my dorm room that morning, but I still haven't told her the particulars of the fight or the fact that I'm training for the next one at Carson's Gym every night after football practice.

I cock my head, thinking. "Okay, my pet peeve is when you're watching a horror movie and that *one* person breaks off from the group to go search. Right then you know that's the next one who's going to end up dead. Why are people so stupid?"

She laughs. "Right! Why don't they just get in their car and go to Starbucks? At least then they wouldn't die." She takes a sip of soda, her red lips curving around the straw. "What's your favorite color?"

"Your sweater color…whatever that is." My gaze lingers on her tits.

She glances down. "Yeah, you can't seem to take your eyes off of it. It's pale blue, by the way."

"In my defense, it's pretty tight," I point out. My voice lowers. "And you look fucking hot in it."

She rolls her eyes. "Okay, if your life is a movie, what's the soundtrack?"

"*Star Wars* theme song."

She frowns. "But there's no words in it. Are you just saying that to get on my good side?"

I arch my brows. "I've already seen your good side, and it's amazing."

She just shakes her head and bites her lip. I've been flirting with her constantly for the past half hour, and I really do only have one thing on my mind: getting her alone. Between class, football, boxing, and Raven, I've barely seen her.

I laugh. "Fine. My theme song would be..." I drum my hands on the table for dramatic effect. "*We are the Champions* by Queen. It's old school but spot-on."

"Why that one?"

I shrug. "I'm a small-town boy, but I'm going places, and I've never stopped fighting to get ahead. Nothing's going to hold me back, and I'll do whatever it takes to get where I want to go. I want to win a football championship next year, and then I want to have a stellar career in the NFL."

She takes that in, absorbing my words. "Football's everything to you."

I nod. "What's your song?" I ask.

"Definitely *Beautiful Day* by U2. It's about life giving you lemons but you still find the good. I try to do that, especially after Nana passed. I came to Magnolia and try to live a life she'd be proud of."

I look at her, feeling emotion shifting inside my chest. Like me, she's experienced death, but being with her and talking with her, I've never been happier.

I jump into the question game. "What's your favorite... position?"

She pushes her glasses up while her top teeth nibble on her

bottom lip. "What do you mean?"

I lean forward. "Don't be coy. You know." I set my napkin down on the table. "Mine is any position with you. I want you so bad right now that I can't even focus on anything else."

A telltale blush steals up her neck to her lovely face.

God. She's everything I want, and I spend most of my time thinking about her.

But, dread tugs at me. I'm worried she'll discover what I'm doing and be disappointed.

I tried a while back, rather feebly, to push her away at the baseball party, but once I saw her crying at the gym because Han was gone, all that went out the window.

She toys with the straw in her drink. "Oh, I know exactly what you meant. I just wanted the question to be clear before I answered it."

"Well?" I picture her back in my bed with my head between her legs while she moans my name out.

"My favorite position is linebacker, of course." She giggles.

I lean forward again, my voice low and husky. "I've just spent the last hour with you pressed up against me trying my damnedest to do some Latin dance because I like you, and now you're just teasing me."

She lets out a shaky breath. "You're bossy."

"You like it."

"I love it," she whispers, her chest heaving. Her tongue darts out and licks her bottom lip. "Does that even make sense?"

Heat fires through my body. "It does when it's the right

person."

Her eyes hold mine. "How's this for a little tease? I have a skirt on so you have easy access. What are you going to do about it?"

Clearly, she is past being nervous with me.

My cock hardens even more and I stifle down a groan. I look around the restaurant, my head spinning. We're sitting in a booth toward the back, but it's definitely not private, and with what I want, I need privacy. I exhale slowly...and have an idea.

I catch her hand. "I dare you to go to the last stall in the ladies' room and wait for me."

"Now?" She blinks. "Why?"

"You know why." I cup her face. "And have your underwear off or there'll be hell to pay, Buttercup."

Her chest rises rapidly, the color in her cheeks flaming. She thinks for a moment then stands rather shakily, gives me a final lingering look, and heads down the darkened hallway that leads to the restrooms.

I give her five minutes before I pull out a couple twenties that more than cover the bill. Rising up, I'm barely able to walk in my tightened jeans, but I manage to make it over there without anyone glaring at the obvious tent in my pants. At this rate, I'm going to bust a button off my britches.

Damn. I'm halfway in love with this girl.

CHAPTER 22

DELANEY

Why am I standing in a bathroom stall, you ask?

Because I want Maverick more than I want air.

My head spins with heat and pure need. He is a rollercoaster, dangerous and exhilarating; my brain is telling me to jump off and save myself, but my heart yearns to ride it to the end to see if I live or die.

I hear the door open and the lock slide into place. My heart pounds. The stall I'm in is hot, my skin is hot, and I just might pass out before he—

The door swings open and it's him.

A quivering breath slips out of me.

I breathe in his masculine scent as he stalks forward and laces his fingers through my hair. His shoulders are broad and taut, as if he's coiled like a tiger and ready to pounce. I know that feeling well. I've been on a tight wire all week, wanting him, worrying about him. For now I lock that away, promising myself I'll come back to it later.

He doesn't speak, just runs his eyes over my face before drifting down to my chest then lingering on my legs. I hold up my purple lace underwear, and he takes them from me with a smoldering look then tucks them in the front pocket of his jeans.

"Good girl."

His eyes come back and capture mine, and I feel weak at the desire I see there. We haven't even kissed and I feel like I'm going to come apart.

My breath comes in shallow pants as he places his hands on my shoulders and strokes them down my arms then back up. His fingers drift to the curve of my waist and back up to cup my face. He's so gentle, and the emotion in his eyes—I gasp at what I see. Is it love burning in his gaze, or is it just passion? I don't know, but right now I'll take whatever he gives.

He kisses me, devouring my mouth with his, nipping at my lips and sighing. One of my hands curls around his neck to pull him closer while the other one plants itself on the hard bulge in his pants. My mouth doesn't want to let him go, and it feels like it's the same for him.

He traces his tongue down my neck to my collarbone, slips his hand under my sweater, and massages my breasts, his fingers tweaking the lace of my demi-bra. I toss my head back and hiss at the pleasure that zips up my spine. He maneuvers my arms out of my sweater and pushes it up around my neck without taking it off. I'm hot with it like that, but I don't care. All I want is *him...this.* My nipples strain toward him and I bite my lip when he finally frees them with a snap of the back clasp. He groans as he cups my bare breasts, his expression raw with passion, visceral and primitive. His mouth sucks at a nipple, making me gasp.

"You're too beautiful for me," he says.

With need and lust rippling through my veins, I try to be careful as I help him take off his t-shirt and sling it over the top of the stall door. Though faint, there are still bruises on his body, and I lean down to kiss each one. A hiss escapes his lips as I trace my fingers over his pink nipples, playing with his skin. My mouth finds them, exploring, tasting him.

I work my way lower to unbutton his pants and shove them down around his hips. I push at his tight athletic briefs, my fingers stroking over the head of his cock. My mouth follows, tasting him the way I've been thinking about all week, and he groans my name.

While my mouth works him, he reaches his fingers underneath my skirt. He finds me wet and grunts as his finger slides back and forth against my core, teasing me and making me squirm with need. I'm panting around him, feeling like I'm going to come any moment.

"Do you have protection?" I gasp out. *Hurry, hurry* is all I can think because it seems like a million years ago that we were together in my bed.

He gives me a quick nod and tugs a package out of the back pocket of his jeans.

I watch him slide it over the bulbous head and onto his hard shaft, the veins there long and thick. His eyes look up at me.

He tugs my neck forward and kisses me, his chest against my breasts. In between kisses he whispers, "You're everything I've ever wanted."

In a rush, he has me picked up as if I weigh nothing. My legs wrap around him, my center resting on his abs. I'm soaked and I don't care that I'm out of control for him.

His length nudges at my entrance, easing inside until finally he grunts and sheaths himself fully. Neither of us move a muscle for ten seconds, our faces next to each other, my hands hanging on to his shoulders.

"Fuck." He closes his eyes and groans as I begin to move on him, grinding my hips and swiveling.

He turns so I'm pressed against the wall then withdraws and slides back in, the fullness intense, a sensation I quickly adjust to as he begins again. Hard and fast is the pace, and I can't get enough. Each time he strokes inside me, it's like it's happening all over again for the first time.

"Mav," I say as he watches me, detailing every nuance of my reaction. I'll never have enough of this, of him. He's ruining me.

I turn my face to him, gasping for air. His lips kiss my shoulder, sucking hard as my body clenches his cock.

Sensation gathers, growing warm and then hot at the base of my spine. Arching my back, I take all of him as his hands hold my hips, pushing me harder and harder until I break, shattering into a million pieces.

I breathe out his name and hang on as his cock swells inside me. He crests over the edge and calls my name.

His mouth finds mine and kisses me, his hands still holding me up as he pushes into me and shudders.

I feel supple and loose, like a cat that's just been fed a big bowl of cream and now only wants to bask in the sun.

Then I'm reminded of where I am: in the restroom of the local Buffalo Bills.

He slowly lowers me. "I can't believe we just did that," I say as I disentangle myself, my feet finding solid ground.

I'm wobbly as I straighten my clothes, watching out of the corner of my eye as he disposes of the condom then zips his pants up. I hand him his shirt and he finishes getting dressed, watching me with a considering look on his face.

"What?" I say, turning to him. I know I must look crazy with my hair everywhere.

"Nothing, just…happy."

Emotion clogs my throat. We're moving so fast, but I can't stop it. *I can't.* I want him. Maybe I love him. My hands shake as I ease past him to open the stall and step out into the sink area where I turn on the faucet and run cold water over my wrists. I don't know why I do it, just that my Nana used to do it when she got flustered. It seems fitting.

He grabs my hands and laces our fingers together. "So are we going back to your place or mine?"

"I thought you said you had to go work out?"

"I do, but I want to hold you tonight. I want to wake up and you be there."

I smile. "Mine."

CHAPTER 23

DELANEY

Mav-Man: Did you get the gift I left on your porch?

Me: You mean the stuffed animal wearing a Jedi outfit? Didn't know it was from you.

Mav-Man: Minx. Who else buys you stuffed cats? I'll make you pay for that remark later.

Me: Can't wait. XOXO

I sip from a glass of red wine as I sit across from Maverick inside Giardina's Italian Grill, an eatery a few blocks from campus. With dark lighting, a ceiling strung with ivy, and a collection of art depicting scenes from Venice on the amber-colored walls, it's quaint and a popular date night place—which is what we're doing tonight. Saturdays are busy, and I'm glad Maverick called ahead to reserve a table for four. I cross my legs under the table and uncross them, nervous to be meeting his dad and seeing Raven again.

He taps his fingers on the table, on edge, perhaps because his dad and sister are officially ten minutes late. He keeps staring at his phone, checking the time and seeing if she's texted him.

I study him, taking in the chiseled jawline, the straight angles of his nose and forehead. It's late March and his hair has grown out; he wears it swept back off his face, the ends curling around his ears. A pale blue button-down shirt with the cuffs rolled up is paired with a pair of jeans that sculpt the taut muscles of his thighs. He smells intoxicating, all earthy and spicy from his shower at my place. Even though he looks great semi-dressed up, my favorite look on him is gym shorts, a tank, and a baseball cap pulled low over his eyes.

"You look gorgeous," he tells me, taking in my demure Peter Pan-collared black dress. The lapels are a stark white with tiny seed pearls I sewed on myself. His hand reaches out and strokes a long finger down my neck, ending at my collar where he tugs me toward him and kisses me lightly on the lips. "I'm with Skye—you should look into fashion when you graduate."

I grin. I love how beautiful and talented he thinks I am. "Maybe. I'm not sure what I'll do after this, maybe grad school."

"Where at?" There's a worry line on his forehead, and I wonder if it's because he doesn't want me to go to far from wherever he ends up in the NFL.

I study the white linen of the tablecloth. "I'm not sure, maybe somewhere back in North Carolina."

What I don't say is I really don't know because I want to know where he'll be going next year. I sigh at the prick of fear that rises up at the direction of my thoughts. Maverick is…he's all I think about. What I felt for Alex doesn't even compare.

Just then his phone pings with a text, and he pulls away to glance down at it.

His face tightens.

"What's wrong?" Just a few days ago, a local strip club called about his dad, and Maverick drove to pick him up then took him back to their house, where he spent the rest of the night. He wasn't able to leave until the nurse showed up for Raven.

He exhales, his eyes still reading the text. "It's Raven. Dad hasn't come home from work yet and isn't answering his phone. The nurse is ready to go but doesn't want to leave her alone. She's gone next door to see if the neighbor is home." He looks up at me. "He should have been home an hour ago." He checks his watch.

"Can you call the garage?"

He grimaces. "They're already closed. He's probably at a bar." Uncertainty crosses his face and he looks around the room as if searching for answers. He's told me a lot about growing up with an alcoholic father who rarely had a steady job.

He looks through his phone and calls a few different numbers to ask if his dad is there, keeping his voice quiet.

I take his hand. "We can just go to her. That way you won't be worried and she won't be upset, and you can figure out what's going on with your dad later."

He looks up. "You don't mind?"

"Of course not. She's your sister." I pause, seeing from his intensity that this is important to him. "I've always wanted a sister, so any sister of yours is a friend of mine," I assure him.

"The trip will take an hour if we go get her then come back —and she *will* want to come back because this is her favorite place. You said earlier you were starving…" He searches my face for a chink in my optimism.

There isn't one.

I smile. "You'll figure out that I'm pretty easy and laid back. I may be a bit of a nerd, but that doesn't mean I'm a control freak and have to have everything a certain way." I gather my purse and jacket off the back of the chair and notice he hasn't moved yet, a hesitant look on his face. "Is there something else?"

He stands and takes my arm in a brisk motion, as if he doesn't want to respond to my question. He lays down more than enough money to cover my glass of wine and gives a nod to the server who brought us our drinks. He explains to her that we have to go but will come back later. A young teen girl who's obviously a Maverick fan, she tells us they'll make sure we have a table once we come back.

"What's wrong?" I ask as we head to the foyer of the restaurant.

He exhales. "The thing is…you've never seen where I grew up. It's not much."

"You don't have to apologize for how you grew up. Your humble circumstances made you who you are"—I squeeze his hand—"and you're one of the most honest, hardworking people I know."

"I'm not honest."

What? I look at him. "Yes, you are."

He doesn't meet my gaze and I imagine I read remorse on

his face, but over what, I can't imagine.

"You *have* stalked me since freshman year…so there's that." I give him a soft slap on the shoulder, trying to change his mood.

He nods and shoots me a brief smile, seeming to come around. "Yeah, and you always dreamed about me even when we weren't together. You watched me on the field at every home game and wondered what it would be like between us. You may not admit it—because you were seeing Alex—but I know you did."

"How on earth do you contain that giant ego of yours? Oh, that's right—you don't."

He tugs at my hair. "Admit it—you've wanted me since the moment I kissed you at the bonfire."

"Nope."

"You have."

"Okay, fine. I can't deny a few fantasies," I murmur. "There's this one in particular where you're in a Han Solo outfit in my front yard holding an eighties-style boom box, trying to woo me."

"Do I have a light saber?"

I grin, waggling my eyebrows. "Oh, yeah, a big one."

He laughs, and I lean my head on his shoulder as we walk out the door, aware that several pairs of eyes are watching us. A few die-hard fans even have their phones out and are snapping pics. A young boy, around eight years old, has been sitting in the waiting areas with his family and comes running up, yelling Maverick's name. He hands him a napkin to scrawl an autograph on and he graciously does so before folding it back into the kid's shirt pocket.

Just as we're almost to his truck, Maverick's phone rings and he looks down at it, sees who's calling, and stops.

"Is it your dad?"

He shakes his head, his face hardening "No, but I need to take this." He hands me the keys. "Go ahead and get in. I'll be there in a second."

I glance at the ringing phone in his hand and the scowl on his face.

"Ryker?" I press.

"No. Just wait for me please." His words are curt, and my body stiffens. I want to ask him what the hell is going on, but he's barely noticing because the phone has all his attention. I watch as he stalks away from me to take the call, going several feet before he answers, his voice hushed.

What is he hiding from me?

I get in the truck, but I turn around to watch him as he paces back and forth, his body language tense as he listens intently to whoever is speaking.

Why is he being evasive? Maybe it's Raven. Maybe it has something to do with the bruises he had or the fact that he's always busy. I chew on my lip as worry settles in my gut. Am I putting my trust in someone who's only going to let me down? What if these sweet moments with him are just stolen bits of paradise that will crumble at any moment?

What if…he breaks my heart?

CHAPTER 24

MAVERICK

On Monday, I wake up tired and worn out in my dorm room. After working out in the ring at Carson's for two hours last night, I ended up going out to the trailer to make Raven dinner and then hung around while she took a bath and went to bed.

Dad was there, and I'm still angry with him for being a no-show at the dinner where I'd planned for him to meet Delaney. I don't know why I thought it was a good idea for us all to have dinner. I guess there's just a small part of me that's still optimistic that he will be a regular dad. Turned out, he went to a bar after work for a few drinks and lost track of time. *Figures.* Delaney and I ended up picking Raven up then having dinner with her at Giardina's, and by the time we brought her home, Dad was already in bed passed out—further proof that Pineview is a great idea.

After showering, I come out of the bathroom and Muffin is sitting on the couch in her underwear and one of Ryker's shirts. A cursory glance around the room tells me his door's shut, and I figure he's still sleeping.

She darts her eyes at me rather furtively as she puts something behind her back, and I study her more intently. Maybe it was her phone. *Whatever.* There's not much to steal here, so I ignore it, and I don't want to ask her too many questions because she might get the idea that I'm interested in her.

I mutter out a greeting as I walk past, keeping my eyes averted from her legs, which she's propped up on the coffee table. She's a sly girl with an agenda, and I'm disappointed Ryker is still into her. To me, it's clear she still wants Alex if the way she chased him at the baseball party is anything to go by.

I make my way to the kitchenette to make a protein drink before class.

"So, you're with Delaney now?" she asks, her nasally voice echoing in the room.

I give her a short nod. "We're dating."

Her lips turn down, her distaste obvious. "I don't know what everyone sees in her. First Alex, and now you—she must be amazing in bed."

My nose flares. Everything she says rubs me the wrong way, and I'm pretty sure the feeling is mutual. "I don't talk about my private life."

A laugh comes out of her. "Oh, you'd be surprised what I know about your private life."

I freeze, my eyes on her face, trying to read the smarmy expression there. "Is that supposed to mean something?"

She shrugs, her eyes hard as they stare right back at me.

"I don't like riddles, Muffin." *And I don't like you.*

"No riddles here, just the fact that everyone loves you and

you're the best player ever…right?" With that she stands, marches back to Ryker's room, and shuts the door.

"Where are you off to? I thought you already had football practice," Delaney asks as I load the dishwasher at her house. Ryker and I came over after class and she and Skye made lasagna for us. As a thank you, Ryker and I cleaned up the kitchen.

She's standing next to me, her gaze zeroed in.

I shrug. "We're going to hit the field house for some weight training." Every word is a lie and feels like a bullet to my gut, but I can't tell her the truth: I'm going to meet with Leslie at Carson's tonight to work out the details of the next fight. He was the one who called me as we left Giardina's.

I want to confide in her, but if I get caught fighting, the less she knows, the better, and damn it's hard to admit I'm a cheater who's breaking rules.

"I made cookies," she tells me rather tartly. "Too bad you're going to miss those."

Han is weaving in and out of her legs, and I reach down to give him a pet so I don't have to look her in the eyes. I'm such an asshole. "Just save me some and I'll get them tomorrow."

"Are you coming over later?"

"No, I have a test tomorrow." I stand and brush my lips across hers. "Thank you for the meal. It was amazing as always."

Feeling the weight of her eyes on me as I move to grab my

gym bag, more guilt settles over me. Besides Raven, she's the most important person in my life, and I'm not giving her what she deserves.

After thanking the girls for dinner, Ryker follows me as I make my way out the front door.

He starts in on me as soon as we get in the truck. Earlier I told him about Leslie calling me, and he's been fuming all afternoon.

"You can't do another fight. I won't let you," he mutters as I start the truck.

I exhale. "Just one more and I'm set to pay for Pineview for an entire year. If I get one more fight in now—before football starts this fall—then I won't have to do it again." I flick a quick glance over to him as he stares out the window, clearly annoyed with me. "Look, think about Raven—this is for her. My dad is shit, man. He can't take care of her, and I'm barely managing everything I have with school and football. Plus, I've already paid the facility the deposit. Raven moves in May 1st."

Knowing she will be happy and safe...that makes it all worthwhile.

"Unless you get caught," he mumbles, raking a hand through his hair. "Then you'll never play pro ball."

"Nothing's been said about the last fight, and no one will find out about this one."

"Secrets never stay secrets, Mav. Someday it's going to come back on you."

"Have you told anyone?" My head recalls Martha-Muffin in our dorm room and how oddly she acted.

"No, of course not." His words are clipped.

My hands tighten on the steering wheel. "If you've got something to say, spit it out."

He exhales loudly. "Have you told Delaney what you're doing for cash? Because she isn't going to be cool with it."

"Stay out of me and Delaney."

"See, you know I'm right. You haven't been honest with her—with anyone, not even Raven."

My teeth clench. "What's your point?"

He waves his hands around. "Raven has a traumatic brain injury, and you're out there getting beat up. Last time you nearly fractured a rib."

I shrug. "It's the same as being on the field."

"On the field, you have a helmet and pads."

I shake my head. "I could break my neck on the football field and never walk again. I could die in a car wreck like my mom. I could be walking across the street and get hit by a car. I can't live my life by what-ifs. All I know is what I have to do right now, and that's take care of my little sister. No one else is going to do it—not my dad, not the state, *me*."

We're both quiet for a moment.

"You don't know what it was like growing up like I did," I add. "I got a job when I was thirteen, mowing the football field at school. When I was sixteen, outside of football, I helped my dad clean Carson's Gym. I've worked my entire life and now I have the chance to really provide for Raven."

He looks out the window.

"Dude, let it go," I say. "Be my friend."

He shrugs. "I just…have a bad feeling."

"Maybe it's because you've been hanging out with Muffin."

He juts out his jaw. "So?"

I sigh. "All I'm saying is be careful. Just a few weeks ago, she was hot and heavy after Alex."

He scratches at his scruff. "We're keeping it casual."

"Good."

We enter the gym and take in the surroundings. It's seven at night but the place is busy. Off to the left are the locker rooms, and I head there to wrap my hands, change into shorts, and put on some flat, high-topped boxing shoes, ones Leslie provided for me after the last fight. I figure I may as well get some sparring in while I'm here.

Ryker goes over to the weights to do some lifting.

I come out of the locker room and see Leslie has entered the building and is in the main office talking to Carson, the owner. Dressed in a suit that looks out of place in the smelly gym, he gives me a wave through the glass walls.

I nod and head that way, and as soon as I enter the room, Leslie motions for Carson to leave us, which I can appreciate. I'm sure Carson knows what's going on, and I don't doubt he's got his fingers all up in this, but I'd rather speak with Leslie alone.

Leslie motions for me to take a seat, but I decline. I don't like him. He's a slimy guy who's taking advantage of the fact that I need money. It makes me wonder about the other players and their reasons for fighting for him. No football player with a good record would do this *just* for the money; it's too dangerous.

"I'll stand, thanks." I cross my arms. I want him to know he doesn't own me. "You said you had some news about the fight," I say.

He studies me with a smile that's overcrowded with small teeth in an otherwise large mouth. "Yes. Same terms as before. Your opponent has knocked out everyone before the second round. You up for it?" His beady eyes rake over me, an arch to his brow as he takes in the additional muscle I've managed to build up in the past couple of weeks. I've also healed up completely and feel like I'm at the top of my game.

"Who is it?" A whole list of names runs through my head, mostly SEC powerhouses since those are the ones I know the best.

"He's an Alabama boy, and the fans are chomping at the bit to get to you. It's all everyone is talking about."

Everyone being his little circle of rabid rich fans.

My lips flatten. Alabama is the best in the country—this year. They defeated us in a tight Rose Bowl game last year, knocking us out of the national championship.

A muscle flexes in my jaw, and I give him a sharp nod. "Done. Just tell me when."

"I'll make the final arrangements and call you." He puts out his hand for me to shake. There's an ostentatious ring on nearly every finger, but I grit my teeth and take it.

Out of the corner of my eye, I see a flash of movement outside the office, and I turn to see Muffin watching us, a petulant look on her face.

I narrow my eyes at her and she flips around then hurries toward the door, but not before I see that she had her phone out.

Did Ryker tell her we were coming here? That doesn't make sense, not when I'm meeting Leslie here.

Brushing past him, I exit the office, my eyes scanning the gym for Ryker, who I find in the back on a butterfly machine.

Everything seems okay, but I know something isn't right. I follow Muffin as she heads to the foyer, her bag slung over her shoulder.

I call her name, but she tears out the front door, a purposeful stride in her walk.

Following behind her, I exit the building and see her half-running to her little Mercedes convertible.

Jogging, I catch her before she gets it unlocked.

"Hey, I didn't know you worked out here." It's not unusual for students to come, especially since the Waylon facility doesn't offer the same variety of classes, but I've never seen her here. "What's up?" I say.

"Yeah, well, I signed up for a CrossFit class here. The only time available is super late." She's fumbling around in her purse for her keys. "I thought it would be great since Ryker is here a lot."

My stomach falls. He must have mentioned that he comes here. *Dammit.* I don't need Muffin sniffing around and seeing me spar in the ring. I mean, it doesn't look bad to box, but still…I want to cover my tracks.

"Oh, did you see him? He was on the butterfly machine."

She blinks. "Uh, no…but I saw you in Carson's office."

My eyes narrow. "Is that right? Huh."

"Yeah, that's right," she says curtly, giving me a sneer.

"You seem a little off, Muffin. You okay?"

With an aggravated sigh, she glares up at me. "Why so many questions, Maverick?"

I sneak a look at the phone she still has clutched to her side and nod my head at it. "Did you take a picture of me?"

She blinks. "What if I did? Is that a problem? Do you have something to hide?"

A scowl pulls my brow down. "No."

She laughs. "I did actually, of you and the fat guy in the suit. Those glass walls are amazing—I could see everything."

I stiffen. "Don't meddle in my life, Muffin. Stick to Ryker." My voice is hard and flat.

She bristles and opens her car door, giving me a cunning look as she slides inside. "Are you threatening me?"

I take a step back, holding my hands up. "No. I'm just asking why you took a picture of me with a man you don't know."

She arches her brow. "There are ways to find out who he is. Ever hear of reverse image search on Google? Besides, I asked Carson and he told me his name was Leslie Brock. Guess who I'm going to look up when I get home?"

I'm baffled by why she would even care.

Anxiety eats at me, imagining her blabbing around campus about who Leslie is. I know exactly what she'll find out if she tries hard enough: he owns casinos.

"Don't start something you don't know anything about," I

say tightly.

An insinuating expression flits over her face. "Just a heads up, Ryker leaves his phone out constantly. I just happened to take pictures of some messages you've sent him that came across his lock screen—texts about fighting in Tunica and a man named Leslie, and then lo and behold, I ask Carson who you're with and he says *Leslie*. Not smart to meet your bookie so close to home."

Fuck. I can't breathe.

I bark out a laugh. "He isn't my bookie."

She's off base, but dangerously close...

"Yeah, right. You've been gambling."

"It's not what you think it is," I say. "I've never gambled."

There's so much more I want to say to her—I want to fucking go off on her—but I'm terrified.

"Whatever. You'll say anything to protect yourself." She's managed to get in her car now. "I'll see you," she says as she slams her door and cranks her engine.

I stand back as she jerks out of her parking spot and squeals off.

Everything feels wrong.

I scrub my face and head back into the gym. I have to find Ryker and figure out what the hell is going on.

CHAPTER 25

DELANEY

It's the Thursday night before spring break and the library is a dead zone, except for the diehards who aren't leaving early for a quick trip to somewhere.

It's seven o'clock, so I have two more hours before I can hightail it out of here and head to my house, where I'm supposed to meet Maverick.

Voices drift in from the front, and I look up from the circulation desk I'm manning, expecting to see my co-worker who's been working on the main floor downstairs, but it's Martha-Muffin and one of her sorority friends.

She sees me and changes her trajectory, making her way over to the desk. She practically flounces in a pair of white cutoffs and a lace top that barely covers her boobs.

I exhale. "Mensa meeting for two tonight? Please don't let me interrupt. Choose a table, any table." *As long as it's far, far away from me.*

"You think you're so smart." She shakes her head. "It all might just fall down around you."

I arch my brows. "*Okaaaay.* Am I supposed to be scared?"

"You would be if you knew what I knew," she says, twisting her lips.

I sigh, not in the mood for her antics. I just want to get out of here and see Maverick. "Unless you're here to check out a book—which I highly doubt is the case—or need help finding a book—which I also highly doubt—then I'll leave you to your ridiculously vague comments and go do something productive with my time."

I skirt around the edge of the counter, my goal to get as far from the toxicity as I can, then I hear her voice calling behind me in a singsong tone. "I know something you don't."

I push my glasses up and turn around. "I already know you slept with my ex. Over and done. I've moved on."

She laughs, but it isn't a pleasant sound, and by now the group of guys back in the corner openly stare at us.

"This is about Maverick."

She's toying with me, I tell myself, but part of me—the insecure side of me—wants to know exactly what she means. My old anxieties tug at me, reminding me that Alex cheated and saying maybe Maverick has too.

"Fuck off, *Martha*."

She rears back in surprise. "Well, you do have claws. I was beginning to wonder."

I flip back around and head down an aisle.

Her parting shot follows me. "Just ask him why he's been training at Carson's Gym so much. Ask him who Leslie is."

Leslie? Is she someone he's seeing at the gym? He's been telling me he goes to the field house to work out…

But I did see him at Carson's all those weeks ago when

Han was lost.

I take the stairs two at a time, her comments niggling at me, digging under my skin. I try to pack them away and store them in a back corner of my mind, but when my phone pings with a text from Maverick and I read it, the uncertainty yanks at me even more.

Rain check on tonight? We've got a big scrimmage coming up and I need the rest.

Fine, I say.

You okay?

I type **Yes**, but then delete it.

I'm not okay, not at all, and I need time to think. I don't respond, instead just tuck the phone back in my pocket.

CHAPTER 26

DELANEY

The next day, Ryker opens the door, this time with some clothes on. It makes sense since it's the afternoon and after classes, but in a dorm with athletes, you never know. I'm here to pump him for information, and I'm not above using food to get what I want.

"Mav isn't here. Already left for the gym."

I let out a sigh. "Is he at Carson's with *Leslie*?"

Ryker pales—just a hair—and I know I'm on the right track. "He might be at Carson's, but I don't know a Leslie."

My heart drops at his obvious lie, but I shrug, playing it cool. "I know he's not here. He texted me this morning and said he had things to do today." He's been too busy for me for the past several days, and my nerves are stretched thin. It feels like whatever we had is slowly slipping away and there's nothing I can do to stop it.

He nods. "So why are you here?"

I pull a full pecan pie out of my handy little Tupperware carrier. "I made pie, and I do recall you mentioning once that pecan is your favorite. Just thought I'd drop it off."

"Man, you're the best." He opens the door wider and I step inside, heading to the kitchenette. "It's been a shit day and I really need this."

"Oh? What's wrong?" Normally he always wears a smile, but now that I'm noticing, there are dark circles under his eyes and his hair is everywhere, as if he's been rubbing it.

His lips tighten. "Just girl problems." Muffin problems, no doubt, but I hold on to that thought and wait.

"Let me cut you a piece," I say as I pull open a drawer to find a pie cutter. Alas, these guys are primitive, so I settle for a butter knife. I slice into the flakey golden crust, tossing a look at him over my shoulder.

"Sure." His eyes are focused on the dish, and I smile at his interest.

"By the way, this was my Nana's recipe, and it's been handed down in my family for generations. It won a blue ribbon at a fair in North Carolina."

He walks in closer. "Awesome, but why are you bringing *me* pie? Shouldn't it be for Mav?"

"Just thought we could chat. Want me to make us some coffee to go with this? Or some iced tea?"

"I think my mom left some Lipton packets here the last time she dropped off groceries, and there's sugar in the pantry. I don't have an iced tea maker though. We can use a pan?"

"Sure." I nod and he helps make the tea, immediately turning on the stovetop. There's a bit of pep in his step, probably excitement about the pie. He fills the pan with water and I drop in the bags as he digs out a pitcher. I mean, I don't really want tea, but I'm nervous and need something to keep my hands busy because I feel guilty about pumping Maverick's friend for information. I exhale. I'm desperate, and I just want Ryker to reassure me that everything's okay.

"Let's talk while the tea brews, yes?"

"Sure." He shrugs.

I set the pie in the center of the table and cut it into six large slices, the sterling silver of the knife slicing into the crystallized pecans and down farther into the dark gooey confection.

"So the recipe is a big secret?"

"Nana thought it was. Sometimes I think it's a shame not to tell people about it because I'm the only person in the world that knows it, and I don't have any family to pass it on to."

"You're not missing much. Family can be a real pain in the ass. Maybe you'll have a house full of kids someday."

I hope so. "Or a bunch of cats."

Silence settles between us as we wait for the tea to brew, and I notice the pensive look on Ryker's face.

I'm trying to figure out how to lead into asking him details about Maverick when he speaks first. "You didn't *really* come here just to bring me this pie, did you?"

I feel myself blush. "Correct."

A gruff laugh comes out of him. "You came to ask me about Maverick and why he's so…weird lately, right?" His eyes flash down to the gooey goodness that's spreading out on his plate. "The pie is a bribe."

He's funny, and I smile a little even though I'm worried. "Pretty much."

He sighs, but I don't think he's annoyed with me.

My stomach churns and I go all in. "The truth is…Muffin came to see me at the library last night, throwing threats around about Maverick and someone named Leslie. Is he cheating on me?"

He shakes his head. "No. God, no—Maverick wouldn't do that. Leslie is a guy, a real piece of work."

I sit back, my head spinning with relief. I'd been so focused on him cheating…

He rakes a hand through his hair, his lips twisting as if he's deep in thought.

"But you're not telling me everything," I say. "What does Muffin claim to know about Maverick?"

He rubs a hand down his face. "This whole Muffin thing… shit, it's my fault. Apparently one night she got my phone while I was sleeping and read a bunch of texts from Maverick. It was on the lock screen but she was still able to take pictures of messages about a casino and this Leslie person. She's crazy. She even went up to him at Carson's and took a picture of him with the guy."

He says a few other things, mostly about how he's pissed at Muffin and how he's tried to call her but she's not answering, but all I can focus on is the casino bit.

My heart drops. "He's been gambling?"

He studies me and frowns, giving me a rueful look. "No, and I've already said too much. I only did because I know you care about him and if anyone can talk to him, it's you. You'll have to ask him for the rest of the story."

I chew on my bottom lip, my head trying to piece it all together. Ryker's right—if I want to know the truth, I'll have to confront Maverick.

He lets out a sigh as his eyes drift back to the plate in front of him. "Are you still going to let me eat this?" The fork is already in his hand and there's a huge clump of crust and pecan filling on the tines.

"Eat the damn pie."

"Thank God." He shoves the huge bite in his mouth and groans so loudly, I blush. Once he gets the first bite down, he reaches across the table and gives my hand a squeeze. "Don't give up on him. Just talk to him."

CHAPTER 27

MAVERICK

I'm leaning against the wall in the gym's showers, letting the hot water run down my body. I've been pushing myself to the limit this week, preparing for the fight along with our first scrimmage game tomorrow. NFL scouts will be in attendance, and just thinking about everything I have on the line kicks up my adrenaline.

I think back to Muffin and what she might do with those text messages she took pictures of. Everything she has is just conjecture, but she's batshit crazy, and batshit crazy can cause a lot of havoc.

I get out and am drying off when I hear the clank of a door somewhere in the building. *Dammit.* I thought Carson locked up before he left, but obviously he was leaving that to me since I'm here so late.

Still damp, I toss on my gym shorts then ease out the door and into the darkened gym. The lights are off and the only light is the glow from Carson's office, which he leaves on all the time.

"Maverick?"

My shoulders sigh in relief—it's Delaney.

My eyes scan over her, eating her up. She's wearing a pair of gray yoga pants and a shirt that says *I'm Sorry For What I Said When I Was Hungry*. Her hair is up in a side knot thing, and strands of blonde hair that have escaped fall down her cheek.

I exhale. Damn, she's beautiful, but she shouldn't be here.

"What are you doing here? It's past eleven."

She looks around the deserted gym, her gaze ending on the boxing ring. She pushes her glasses up on her nose. "Muffin came to see me at the library last night, and I went to see Ryker today. He didn't tell me everything, so I'm left piecing things together. I'm not sure what to think, and I'm here to find out what the hell is going on with you."

"Okay." I swallow as my entire body tenses. My chest feels like a chunk of ice.

"Who's Leslie and what does he have to do with a casino?"

Fuck. My pulse kicks up, dread filling my gut as I realize the one person I didn't want to know what I'm doing is about to find out what a liar I am. I suck in a sharp breath, gathering myself.

"Let me get dressed first," I say before turning back around to head into the locker room, trying to keep it together. She follows me as I march away and dig through my gym bag, my eyes avoiding hers.

"Is that how you want to play this? By not saying anything?" I look up and her hands are on her hips, her breasts straining against the fabric of her shirt.

I slip a Waylon football shirt over my head and shove my

feet into Adidas slip-ons. "I just didn't want to involve you. The less I say, the better." My voice is soft.

Her hands fall to her sides and she clenches them. "You've been lying to me for weeks. I thought we…had something real." She swallows, her eyes searching my face for answers. "Don't we?"

"I don't know. This isn't the time to ask me, Delaney." It hurts to say the words, but I'm reacting on instinct. I need to push her away and just focus on the game tomorrow.

She stiffens. "Who are you?"

I scrub my face. "Look, my life…it's crazy right now, and I don't want you caught up in my shit."

"With this Leslie person?" Her voice trembles, and I know her well enough to know she's close to tears.

"Yes."

"What? Is he like a mobster or something? Do you owe him money?"

I push my hair off my face, tugging on the ends. *Fuck it—just tell her.* "No, I'm fighting in Tunica for him. He owns a couple of casinos. Muffin thinks he's my bookie, but he's not."

Her chest rises rapidly and she looks faint. She sits down on one of the benches.

"I'm just fighting. I get in the ring, go a few rounds, and get paid a flat fee if I win. That's it."

She sucks in a shuddering breath as the dots are connected in her head. "That's why you were all beat up before?"

I nod.

She shakes her head. "But you can't take money from anyone, not if you want to play football."

An eerie calmness settles over me. "I know."

"Why?" She stands and walks over to me, her hands fluttering as if she's a caged bird who needs to escape but doesn't know the way out.

I close my eyes and take a deep breath. "I did the fight for Raven, to pay for Pineview."

She blinks, taking that in. "I didn't realize you were paying the bill. I thought the state or insurance was."

"No." My shoulders slump as I feel the weight of all my decisions. "I'm sorry for lying to you. I've been coming here to spar as much as I can. I just wanted to keep you out of it in case the press finds out."

She stares at me, taking it all in.

I pick up my gym bag. "I need to go. The scrimmage is tomorrow and I have to be rested. It's late. I'll see you later?"

Hurt flashes over her face, and her eyes shimmer. "Seriously?"

I nod. "The NFL scouts are coming. I need some space, okay?"

She nods, pain in her eyes as they dart around the room. "Fine. I see what's most important to you." She brushes past me and out the door.

Part of me wants to call her back, for her to just…help me through this craziness, but the other part knows I need distance. I need to focus on tomorrow and everything else that may come with it.

CHAPTER 28

MAVERICK

The next day, I'm on the way to the field to dress out for the scrimmage.

I was up late thinking about Delaney, and I'm beat. At least Eminem is blaring on the radio, and I crank it up. The lyrics to "One Shot" blast out as I tap the beat on the steering wheel. The song feels prophetic. The NFL scouts will be sitting in the stands getting a tight view of me as I manage the defense, and whatever happens will definitely set the tone for next year.

I pull into the parking lot and make my way to the dressing room. Most of the guys aren't here yet, and more than likely won't be for another hour. I like to come in extra early, get dressed, and get myself mentally prepared for the game. Every hardcore player has a few game-day quirks, and mine is running my hands along the turf or grass before any other player steps on it. Ryker likes to tell everyone I actually eat the grass, but that's a lie. Still, I go along with it, let them think I'm crazy. As for Ryker…his is getting bitch-slapped by one of the coaching assistants while I hold his hands behind his back. Says it gets his adrenaline going.

Coach Alvarez comes out of his office and meets me in the hallway. A few inches shorter than me with a bald head and bright blue eyes that don't miss a thing, he's in his forties and stocky. A former WU player, he lives and breathes the game. His face is grim most of the time, as if the weight of the world is on his shoulders, but today there's an extra bit of downturn at the corners of his mouth. Known for his profanity and booming voice, he scares the shit out of most people, and no one wants to get on his bad side. He can rake you over the coals faster than a quarterback sneak.

I nod. "Coach. On my way to the locker room."

"My office first, Monroe." He juts his chin in the direction of his door.

My first thought is *Shit, he knows,* and a wave of dread washes over me. He's been nothing but kind to me, a good coach who saw right away that I had no father figure at all, and freshman year, he made sure to check in with me from time to time.

My second thought is that this is a pep talk. He knows how much I'm hanging on to the fact that the scouts are interested in me, especially since I didn't go out early. They want to see if I'll live up to the hype.

I follow his broad frame into his office. Boxes of equipment, helmets, and padding are stacked against the walls, and a white board and a projector sit in the back surrounded by several desks and chairs. This is the coaching headquarters where the assistants meet to decide how we're going to be playing the game. He leans against his desk.

"Shut the door."

I close it as quietly as I can, suddenly a ball of nerves.

"Take a seat."

His voice is hard as nails—the usual.

His eyes bore into mine, that deep frown on his face, making his chin triple as it digs into his chest. A long stretch of ten seconds goes by as a myriad of emotions cross his face, ones I can't read...don't want to read.

My hands shake as I clasp them in front of me. "Sir? Is everything okay?"

"No, Monroe, everything is not fucking okay." His voice is deadly quiet.

That's when I know it's bad. He's not yelling, and this is even worse than if he were.

"I want to know why the motherfucking hell I got a call from the athletic director this morning about an anonymous tip that you're somehow involved in gambling."

It's not just my face that pales—it's my entire body. I feel my skin grow cold. I lick my lips.

"I don't know anything about that, sir."

"Don't fucking play with me, son. Have you been gambling?"

I feel faint.

I tell the truth. "Sir, I have not been gambling. I would never gamble on a game or throw a game. Winning—this team —means everything to me."

He squints at me, a scrunched up look on his face as if he's tasted something sour. "Then where the hell is the AD getting this from?"

"A girl, Coach. She thinks she knows shit and she doesn't."

I grip the edge of my chair. Part of me wants to tell him every-thing…

Tell him, my inner voice screams as nausea washes over me. *Let out the guilt you've been carrying.*

But…I'd never play for him again.

"Son, are you sure you're telling me everything? The AD says I'm supposed to question you, but if you got nothing, I'll let you play today. It is a big fucking day."

I feel the weight of his stare and it makes my heart jerk.

What I've done is so goddamn wrong.

I should just quit football and get a job and support me and Raven. I can live at the trailer with her and take care of her. I can get a job.

I exhale. I don't want to hang on to this any longer. "The truth is—"

"Al!" It's the quarterback coach at the door, and his eyes go from me to my coach. "Oh, sorry. Am I interrupting anything?"

Coach Al moves off his desk, sticks out his hand, and hauls me up to my feet. "We done here?"

"Uh…"

He gives me a nod and a shove toward the door. "Get the hell out of here, get dressed, and hit the field. I want you out there shining today for the scouts—no matter what. You've told me everything I need to know right now. You got me?"

His gaze brushes over me, dismissing me as he turns to talk to the quarterback coach, but there's a question in his gaze. I realize he likely knows there may be some truth to what was reported to the AD, but he doesn't *want* to know. If he knows, he's culpable. If he doesn't know, I can play today—and I have to play today.

Maybe I'm reading too much into it.

Maybe I'm just paranoid.

Maybe I'm just fucked up.

I picture what things would look like if I didn't have football, and I want to run as far away from Coach as I can.

I can't tell him.

I give him a brief nod and slide out the door.

CHAPTER 29

DELANEY

Skye, Raven, and I weave our way through the crowd of people to get to the section of seats reserved for players' family members. I told Maverick weeks ago I'd make sure Raven saw the game, and that's what I'm doing.

I think back to Maverick and swallow down the lump in my throat as I recall our conversation last night. I still feel like I can't breathe. I'm worried about him, but I'm also angry.

I force a smile, trying to put on a brave face.

With a quick survey of the nearby seats, I find a collection of six men, all dressed in various forms of suits that look a bit too posh for rural Mississippi. They're sitting on the front row at the fifty-yard line, and several of the coaches from Waylon are shaking their hands—must be the scouts. I send up a prayer that Maverick does well.

Waylon's team has been divided up into two separate teams, red and blue, and the winner gets bragging rights for a year plus a party tonight in their honor.

Maverick and Ryker are both on the red team, and when Maverick's name and stats are called, Raven jumps to her feet and claps furiously. I stand up with her and we root for the hometown boy.

Even though my heart aches, my eyes can't get enough of him as he takes the field.

Skye rolls her eyes but stands anyway. "I really don't see what all the fuss is about." Her eyes drift over the players as they line up on the field, seeming to linger a little on Alex. "Guess I like a more trim look."

"Football…is…king," says Raven, and I grin behind my popcorn.

Skye laughs. "Well, aren't you just the little spitfire?"

Raven turns her head to Skye. "Spitting…is…gross."

"It means you're sassy and smart," I add.

Raven grins, her big eyes finding mine.

I nod.

Raven leans over on her knees, propping her chin up, laser focused on the team as they line up. Maverick barks out encouragement and when the blue team snaps the ball, his team flows into motion and tackles the quarterback.

Two more downs, and each time the red team stops the running game before blue can get the ten yards needed for a first down.

"He's…good," Raven murmurs as she crams a handful of candy into her mouth.

"The best," I say, running my eyes over those sure, confident shoulders. He's the focal point of every eye in the stands.

"He…deserves…best," she adds slowly, and I look at her with interest, noting the quiet tone of her voice.

"Of course he does. You do too."

She squints up at the sun that's beating down on us. April in Mississippi can either be humid or freezing, depending on God's sense of humor, and today he must be happy because it's a beautiful seventy degrees.

"I...know...what...he's...doing...is...wrong." Her hands twist at the box of Skittles.

I stop chewing my popcorn. *Does Raven know something?*

"What's he doing that's wrong?"

A pensive look crosses her face. "Heard...phone...call... at...my...house."

"About what?"

"Fighting...football...players...in...casino."

Skye's eyes have widened and she puts her phone down, a confused expression on her face. "No, a casino is where people go to gamble—"

I clear my throat, cutting her off. I haven't said a word to her about what I know. "There's no casino here, and no fighting, I promise." Skye nods then turns back to the game, and I grab Raven's hand. "Don't worry about Maverick, okay?"

She nods, and I turn to watch him run off the field.

I keep my eyes on the game, but my brain flies. I'm sure Raven will keep this to herself, but Martha-Muffin is going to be a problem. How much longer before she tells someone? How much longer before it all hits the fan?

The game is over and I wait near the team entrance to the locker room, just outside the tunnel at the end zone. Maverick comes running out, wearing a pair of slacks and a blue button-down shirt with the cuffs rolled up, obviously dressed up to see the scouts at the meet and greet, and then he'll be off to the party at the AD's house.

He's stopped at a couple of young boys wanting autographs who've been standing here with me for the past half hour. Skye and Raven have gone on ahead, and I don't plan on being here long. I've made up my mind to say what needs to be said, and once it's out, I'm done.

"Congratulations on the win and a great game," I say as he nears me, stopping within a few yards.

He runs a hand through his hair. "Yeah, I played well."

I huff out a laugh at his honest assessment. There's no pretense to Maverick when it comes to his abilities. He looks around for Raven.

"Don't worry, they're waiting for me. We're going to get pizza."

He nods. "Thank you for today. She really wanted to come, and my dad…well, you know how that goes."

"Yeah. I'll make sure she gets home okay."

"Thank you. I appreciate it."

I nod, my emotions tugging at me, clogging up my throat. I swallow. "I also wanted to tell you that I…I don't think we should see each other for a while. You're not being truthful with me, and you haven't been for weeks. Also, I'm not even sure how you feel about me, and if you can't talk to me or tell me what's going on with you, something isn't right." I take a big breath. "We need a break." There, I've said the hard words, and I turn to leave before the tears that are brimming in my eyes fall.

"Delaney, wait!" he calls out as I walk hurriedly across the field. He catches my hand and turns me around. "I'm sorry," he says softly. "For putting you through this, for Muffin hounding you, for lying about the bruises…"

I bite my lip, not able to stop the admission. "For making me fall in love with you?"

"Delaney?" His voice is torn and he swallows. "Is that true?"

God, yes. I do love him. Maybe I have since the moment he admitted he was He-Man. Maverick is in my blood, my skin, my bones. He's the light, the sun I want to orbit.

But, I make mistakes when it comes to love—every damn time.

This time, it hurts way more than it did when Alex cheated on me.

If Maverick cared about me, he'd have told me he loves me back by now instead of just standing there with an uncertain look on his face.

"I always fall for the impossible guy." I clench my hands, trying to keep it together.

He scrubs his face. "Delaney, I'm sorry."

He's sorry?

I close my eyes at the words he's not saying, at the way he isn't committing to us.

"I hear everything you're *not* saying, Maverick—everything."

"Just let me take care of this thing with Raven, and then I'll be back for you."

I sigh. I want to believe him, but still, it isn't enough. "Whatever you're doing—this fighting—you need to stop. It's wrong." I shake my head. "When people care about each other, life has a way of working out. We can figure out Raven's situation together."

A male voice calls Maverick's name from the tunnel, and I shift my gaze to see one of the scouts waving for him to come over.

"Look, I have to head out. Can I come by your place later?"

I shuffle my feet, and his eyes watch me with a desperate look, but I'm not sure he actually feels that way. I just don't know if I'm *worth* it to him…not like he is to me.

"I'm driving down to Panama City tonight with Skye for spring break."

"That didn't take long," he says, a muscle flexing in his jaw. "You're just going to leave me here."

"You wanted space, and now you have it," is my reply, recalling words he said last night.

"Delaney…"

But I don't want to hear anything else. I flip around and stalk off, feeling his eyes on me the entire way.

Before I get far, he calls out, "We aren't over, Delaney, not by a long shot. I'm going to make you proud of me."

I clench my hands into fists and keep walking, because if I don't, I'm going to turn right back around and run straight into his arms and tell him I'll stick by his side. I want to tell him that no matter how many times he pushes me away, I'll always be there.

But I don't.

CHAPTER 30

MAVERICK

Watching her walk away from me nearly makes my knees buckle. It feels like she isn't coming back.

She loves me.

She loves *me*, even though I lied to her.

I've wanted her to say it so many times, yet I'm the one who can't admit what's going on inside me.

"Maverick? You coming?" It's one of the scouts, and I give him a nod and head that way.

Something's got to give. I hate this feeling, like I'm torn apart and in shambles.

I pull out my phone and type a quick text to Delaney.

Don't go to the beach. Please, don't leave me. Just wait.

But, I delete it before I hit send. *Shit.*

What am I going to do?

I think about Raven and how much she loves Pineview, the expression on her face when I told her I got her in.

There are only two options: admit I've been taking money for fighting and lose everything, or just keep my head down, keep on trucking, and pray to God Muffin shuts up.

My head tells me to keep trucking, to maintain the status quo.

But…

I rub at my chest, a nagging, aching feeling tugging at me, telling me I'm going to lose everything.

CHAPTER 31

DELANEY

Even though I told Maverick I was leaving that night, I still half-expected him to show up to catch me before I left. He didn't. I checked and re-checked my phone, hoping to get a text from him, but nothing.

Skye and I made the drive to the beach in five hours. There were other people from Waylon on their way, all of them taking flights or driving, several of them staying in the same area of hotels on the beach.

Two days in and I'm lying out on the sand, wearing a yellow bikini, still a little burned from yesterday's time in the sun, but I really don't care. I'm nursing a bit of a hangover from the shots of Fireball Skye made me take last night. Okay, she didn't make me, but she did strongly encourage me, and I didn't need too much urging after still not hearing anything from Maverick.

A shadow drops down next to me, and I glance up from the book I'm reading, expecting to see Skye, who ran in to grab me a water and get a margarita for herself.

My eyes widen as I take Alex in. I'm not too shocked to see

him here since it's the same place we come every year, but I haven't thought of him in so long that, well, I'm taken back.

Wearing a pair of salmon-colored Ralph Lauren swim trunks, he's tan with a hint of a slight sunburn on his shoulders. He's sitting on the beach lounger next to me, the ones only hotel guests are allowed to sit in, looking quite comfortable as he looks at me.

"Alex? What are you doing here?"

He smiles. "Hey. I texted Skye and she told me where you guys were staying."

Interesting. He and Skye had lunch together a few times last week.

I sit up and ease my sunglasses off, propping them on my head where my hair is tied up in a messy bun. I'm without makeup and my eyes are puffy from crying into my pillow last night.

He tilts his head down toward the north end of the beach. "A couple of guys from the team are staying in a house a few resorts up."

"Cool." I really don't have much to say; I'm too depressed and just *blah.*

"Skye says you and Maverick are having problems?" He squints at me.

"Maybe."

His eyebrows go sky high. "Well, you are at the beach without him."

I nod, feeling the pressure of the headache I've been nursing since I woke up this morning. I slip my sunglasses back down. "He broke my heart. Happy?"

He frowns. "Of course not, but it does explain his bad mood after the scrimmage."

I stiffen, worried. "Did something happen?"

"Yeah. He and the AD exchanged words, and then Maverick left the party."

"He left? *Why?*" My heart is in my throat. *Did he tell them about the fighting?*

Alex looks up at me. "I don't know, but there are rumors going around the team. Nothing concrete, but I've heard gambling tossed around."

I stand up. "He has never gambled! It's your friend *Muffin* who's stirring this pot." I'm glaring at him. "You really know how to pick 'em, Alex. She's a liar and a lunatic."

He holds his hands out in a placating manner. "Look, Muffin is nothing to me, and I'm just telling you the rumor, that's all." He stares at me. "I only want the best for you, and if Maverick is what you want, then I want you to be together—I really do."

I sigh and sit back down. "She hates Maverick…and me, and…" I let my voice drift off. It's not my story to share, and the less that's said about the fighting, the better. "You can't trust her."

"I know."

Skye appears with a sardonic expression as she juggles a cooler and a margarita. Her red hair is a riot of curls around her face, and a sheen of sweat covers her forehead.

"Well, well, well, if it isn't Mr. Silver Spoon."

Alex grunts. "If it isn't Miss I Only Date Baseball Players." He goes to help her with the cooler.

Skye watches him critically as he situates it between the two loungers, underneath the two umbrellas so it doesn't get hot.

"Nice job, Cheater."

"You're welcome, Home Run."

Skye snorts. "You're such a douchebag. You wish you could get a home run."

Alex brushes at a patch of nonexistent sand on his chest. "You wish I'd try."

Oh. My. God.

I forget my own melancholy as I watch their bantering like I'm at a tennis match.

Skye and Alex? I blink. *Wow.* My best friend and my ex might actually have some chemistry.

I look at Alex. "So you wanna hang with us girls today or do you have a hot babe to get back to at your beach house?"

"I'm free."

Skye smiles and bumps him out of the way with her hips as she grabs me a water out of the cooler. "Here, sweetie, for your headache."

Impulsively, I grab her and give her a big hug. She's been waiting on me hand and foot and giving me pep talks for the past few days.

Alex is watching us as I set her down. "Nothing like seeing two chicks rubbing up on each other at the beach."

Skye darts over and tackles him, and I laugh.

Maverick's face comes to mind, and I bite my lip, hoping wherever he is, everything is okay.

CHAPTER 32

DELANEY

"Let's watch a movie!" Skye calls out as we walk in the door of our hotel room.

"It's two in the morning!" is my reply.

She shrugs and bats her lashes at me. She looks at Alex, who's clearly had too much to drink judging by the way he's weaving.

I blow out a breath. *Ugh.* I'm not even buzzing, yet somehow she and Alex are like the Energizer Bunny, still ready to party.

They've worn me out dancing, and all I want to do is crash. It's the only way I can turn my head off and stop thinking about Maverick.

They follow me into the room and I head to the mini fridge to grab water.

"Get me a glass of wine, will ya?" Skye requests as she points herself in the direction of the bathroom. Her face is flushed and lined with sweat from dancing. Knowing her and her penchant for cleanliness, she's headed in there to spritz on more deodorant and powder her nose.

"Red or white?" I ask, looking at the two boxes of wine we bought at the liquor store.

"White."

I give her a nod as she stumbles into the restroom, already fluffing her red hair as she walks in.

"Alex? You want anything?" I ask.

He turns his gaze from watching Skye to me, and I bite back a smirk. Maybe a normal person would be jealous about their ex sending lingering looks their best friend's way, but I'm not. He made a mistake with Muffin, but maybe he learned from it.

"Um, I'll take a wine too," he says. He flops down on the bed spread-eagled, his hand over his face. I'm beginning to wonder how he's going to make it back to his house.

After chugging half the bottle of water, I get to work on making their drinks. Once I have them ready, Skye still isn't out of the bathroom, and I make a mental note to check on her.

I walk over to Alex and nudge him with my hand after setting his drink on the nightstand. "Dude, wake up."

I get nothing but a soft snore.

Dammit.

I decide he's Skye's problem and once she comes out of the bathroom, she can decide what to do with him. He's on her bed, so she should be the one to deal with him.

There's an abrupt knock at the door, and I figure it's the pizza guy from the place across the street. Skye called in an order right as we left the club, and even though it's late, my stomach grumbles.

I fling open the door with cash in my hand and freeze.

Maverick is standing there in the hallway, his head bent as he stares at the floor. There's a slump to his shoulders that breaks my heart.

His head flies up and his eyes are haunted.

"Delaney." My name on his lips is like a benediction to my ears. I've missed him so much, and it's only been a few days. I want to run to him, cup his cheeks, and take that anguish off his face.

A heavy exhalation comes from his mouth as he straightens. "God, thank fuck. I had to bribe the desk clerk and sign three autographs to get your room number, and I still wasn't sure he told me the truth."

"Are you okay? Is anything wrong?"

His eyes cloud over. "Everything's wrong. I came here to —"

His voice abruptly cuts off as he looks over my shoulder into the room where he has a clear view of a set of feet on Skye's bed.

He walks in, brushing past me. "Who the fuck is in your room?" He halts mid-stride, his face paling as he sees Alex. I send up a prayer that he's still out and doesn't have a clue that a hulking man is glaring at him like he wants to yank him up by his ankles and toss him over the balcony.

Maverick's chest heaves, his face oddly still as he moves his gaze around the room, taking in the clothes strewn about on the floor, the shoes I kicked off as soon as I came in, and the boxes of wine. He swallows, his throat bobbing as his eyes finally land on me. His fists are clenched at his sides, a barely contained force about to blow.

"Alex? Seriously? Goddammit, Delaney. You really had me fooled."

I die at his words. The world stops.

I want to rewind everything and make sure Skye doesn't beg Alex to walk us to our room. I wish I'd never even spoken to Alex at the beach today.

He brushes past me and I grab his arm, making him come up short. Anger works his face, and another girl might worry that he'd lash out, but it's Maverick and I know underneath all that muscle is a heart that would never hurt a girl, not even Muffin.

"It's not what you think. Skye and I went clubbing with him then he came up here and promptly passed out. That's it."

His teeth snap together, his shoulders stiff and defensive as he glares at me. I see pain there, hurt. "You tell me you love me one minute and the next you're at the beach with your ex—what am I supposed to think?"

How on earth do I explain to him that Alex doesn't even register on my radar anymore? Not after falling for Maverick.

"You're supposed to believe me because nothing compares to you," I say, letting his arm go. "Because my heart is yours and always will be."

He's made it to the door but turns back toward me. Maybe it's my words that stopped him. He scrubs his face and pulls the hair off his forehead, holding on to it as he stares at me. "You're killing me, Delaney. I can't think straight without you."

We hear Skye then, flushing the toilet then singing "Let It Go" from the *Frozen* soundtrack over the rush of the sink as she washes her hands.

I walk over to him, eliminating the distance between us. "You came all this way, Maverick. Stay and talk to me. Alex... he and Skye...I think there's something there between them— that's why I agreed to go out with them tonight. He's not a rebound guy. I think they like each other. You...you're all I want."

He stares at me for a long time, even after Skye pops out of the bathroom and weaves over to me. She throws her arms around me and once she sees Maverick, she takes a step back, nearly falling. "Whoa. Is there a hot guy that looks like Maverick in our room?" She squints. "Is he a stripper? Please tell me it's a stripper."

"No," I tell her firmly. "It's Maverick."

She blinks. "How did he get here? Is he magic?"

"I drove," he says tightly.

He must be exhausted.

"Well, howdy do, Maverick. I'm glad you're here because this girl has been crying her eyes out." She shakes her finger at me and giggles.

I exhale. "That's enough. You need to go to bed."

"Fine." She burps and pulls her dress over her head like she's getting ready for bed. I try to stop her but she's already got it around her neck, and at this point, I just help her get it off. Tomorrow she'll be mortified that she took her dress off in front of Maverick.

She looks around the room and finds Alex. Her eyes light up then she gets on the bed and lies next to him, her body curling around his. At least she's got a camisole and undies on.

She gives us a little wave. "Peace out, y'all. I got what I need."

Skye says exactly what she thinks when she's been drinking.

"See," I say, looking at Maverick.

There's a tightness around his eyes. "Come here," he says, motioning for me to come closer.

I do, and he curls his arm around me, staring deep into my eyes. "I believe you." He pushes a strand of hair behind my ear, his hand warm as I lean into it. "But if you think for one minute I'm letting you stay in this room with them, you're crazy."

"What do you suggest?"

"Get your shit. You're coming with me."

"Lead the way," I say after grabbing my purse. I don't need anything else, only him.

We make it to the elevator and I don't even ask where we're going. I don't care. As long as I'm with him, everything else will work itself out.

We exit and he leads me to another hotel room, where he slides the key card in the slot and ushers me inside.

Neither one of us speak as we face each other. I'm scared. He looks so serious, the chiseled lines of his face etched with an unnamed emotion.

"Talk to me."

He closes his eyes then opens them again. "I love you, Delaney. I love you so damn much, and watching you walk away from me and not being able to do the right thing for you...I never want to go through that again."

I bite my lip, holding in the swell of feeling that washes over me. "Never again," I whisper.

"I'm sorry I couldn't tell you how I feel after the game. I'm sorry for dragging you into this mess. My life is probably ruined, but right now, I don't even care because all I can think about is you. I can't lose *you*."

I run to him, he catches me, and we kiss. His lips are everything, hot and needy, tasting of a passion that only comes once in a lifetime. Our tongues tangle, greedy for the other, anxious to get our fill.

In a blink, his hands have expertly unzipped my dress and I've removed his shirt. In between long breathy kisses, we hold each other, rushing and touching and taking everything.

It feels like it's been months since I've seen him and I want to relearn his skin, but right now all I focus on is how much I want him inside me.

"Fast now. Slow later," he says as he tugs down my underwear to my heels. He looks up at me from where he's kneeling on the floor and I bite my lip. He's perfect. He's gorgeous with those steel eyes looking right at me.

His lips and tongue kiss my calf, my kneecap, and the inside of my thigh while his hands cup my ass, pulling me closer.

I huff out a laugh. "I thought you said fast."

"I lied," he says breathlessly as his thumbs slide to the front to part me, his tongue lapping. He inhales my scent, his fingers dancing across my body, strumming me and making me undulate against him.

I tug him up. "Maverick...please."

He stands and removes his jeans and shoes, his gaze never wavering from mine. "I didn't bring a condom. I wasn't thinking. I just needed to get to you. I'm clean."

"I'm protected," I tell him, and before I even finish, he's kissing me.

It's perfect.

It reminds me of the night we met at the bonfire when he brushed his lips across mine and became the one I'd never forget. Two stars in the sky, two souls destined to be together.

He picks me up, my legs wrapping around his waist. He likes me like this, and it makes me smile to know the power I have over him.

Holding me around the waist, making it seem almost effortless with his strength, he slides into me slowly, giving me what I need. I gasp each time he takes me, my head leaning against the wall. Our breathing is loud, the sex louder, and I come fast, my legs locking on his hips as I clench around him. We kiss and he breaks with me, our love the perfect storm, a tsunami that washes over us.

Later, we're in bed under the covers, our bodies sated. His fingers trace loops and intricate swirls on my back as he hugs me from behind.

"I told Coach and the AD the night of the meet and greet."

The enormity of his words hit me. "What? Why? Does this mean you aren't going to fight?"

He nods. "Yeah."

I cup his cheek. "What's going to happen to Raven?"

A hint of sadness crosses his face before he recovers. "I don't know."

I kiss him softly on the neck. "I'm sorry I didn't ask sooner."

A brief smile flashes. "We had other things going on."

"Are you okay? I mean, what's going to happen with football?"

He plays with a piece of my hair and doesn't answer.

"Maverick? You seem rather calm about all this. This is your career on the line."

He nods. "I know."

"So?"

He arches a brow. "Will you still love me if I don't play in the NFL?"

"Hell yes," I say.

"That's the answer I was looking for." He gives me a lingering kiss, making me grab his shoulders and pull him down until he's on top of me.

He clasps my hand tight, intertwining our fingers as he looks down at me. "I actually have a plan," he says.

I wrap my hands around his nape and pull his lips to mine. "Whatever it is, I'm in."

We kiss more, our hands exploring. I'm so happy to have him back, but I know we need to talk. No matter what, as long as we're together, we can weather any storm.

CHAPTER 33

MAVERICK

We're at a television station and Coach Al and I sit behind a table, the cameras locked and loaded, ready to film. On my right is Delaney, and on the other side of her, slightly off camera, is Raven. A rep from the NCAA is on the other side of Coach, and we're about to go live on ESPN for an interview about the fighting scandal that's rocked the college sports world since I came forward and admitted to my involvement.

Fred Moran is the interviewer, and he's eyeballing me critically. A former linebacker from Ole Miss, he was one of my heroes when I was a kid, and now he's looking at me like I've disappointed him.

I get that, but I'm ready—ready to be true to everyone I care about.

The interview starts with the control room replaying a statement I made at Waylon that was recorded at a press conference put on by the school then released to the media.

"I fully admit to accepting money for fighting a rival football player. I knew this went against NCAA rules of accepting money for gain. I also take full responsibility for deceiving my university, my teammates, and the people I care about, and for this, I'm deeply sorry."

I didn't reveal Kai's name, leaving it up to him and anyone else who'd been involved to come forward. Sure enough, five additional players also made statements after mine.

Even so, I was the big one, the famous player with so much promise, the one who was going to break out of the small town.

I was a disappointment to everyone—everyone except Delaney, Raven, and Ryker, who've stood by me the entire time.

The cameraman starts a countdown, signaling that we're about to go live.

I tense, and Delaney squeezes my hand.

I look down at her, and she gives me a soft smile. "Me and you, He-Man. We got this."

Fred Moran focuses in on me. He gives me a nod then speaks to the millions of viewers. "As many of you know, Maverick Monroe came forward with a scandal that was hard to believe: a star college football player fighting in a casino for money. That's right, tonight in the hot seat, we have none other than Maverick himself."

The camera swings to me, and I nod and straighten my shoulders. I have nothing else to lose.

"Good evening, Fred." I smile, digging deep for that Maverick charm I used to have. "Before we begin, I'd just like to say I'm a huge fan of you and your career, and I follow this show religiously." I huff out a laugh. "Especially lately since I seem to be the topic of many of your conversations."

He smirks. "People aren't saying very nice things about

you."

I nod. "And I accept that."

His eyes scrutinize me, noting my hand clasped with Delaney's. His gaze brushes over Raven, who smiles at him.

He clears his throat. "I was wondering if perhaps you'd like to shed some light on why you risked your career."

"I didn't do it for the money. I mean, I did, but it wasn't for me. It was for my sister."

He nods, encouraging me to go on.

"In a car accident that took my mom, she suffered a traumatic brain injury, and I've been unable to get proper care for her, the kind she needs. My father is an alcoholic and at times is...unable to care for her, and I was often either in class or at practice."

"He...cooks," Raven calls out, and the camera swings to her.

Fred smiles. "You're Raven?"

She nods and plays with her hair, her voice slow but careful as she speaks. "He...takes...care...of...me."

I give her a soft smile and continue. "As you know, I'm not allowed to work or accept any kind of loan or money from anyone in case it's construed as bribes for football. I was hoping I could get by until the draft next spring. Unfortunately, I'd already opted out of the draft this year when we realized she needed extra care."

Fred exhales. "I see. Do you gamble, Mr. Monroe?"

Ah, the crux of the matter.

"I have never gambled, and Leslie Brock has already told the NCAA that." I go on to tell them the details of the organization, how Leslie's casino is a legit business and I merely worked as an employee.

"I never placed a bet on myself or a fight or a football team. What I did was fight, that's it."

"How much money did you get for the fight?" is Fred's next question.

"Fifty thousand, and every penny went to the facility to take care of Raven."

Raven is crying softly, and Delaney hands her a tissue then pats her on the shoulder. They've grown close these past few weeks.

Fred nods, a softening to his face. "Is it true that you requested the money you'd already paid to the facility be returned?"

I smile. "Yes. We donated the money to fund an animal shelter in Magnolia. It was Raven's idea. She's going to be volunteering there some."

Raven glows at my words.

Really, that was all Delaney. She sat down with Raven and they talked about what kinds of volunteer work she'd like to do. It was something I'd never thought of, mostly because I'd have to get her there and back.

"And what about your sister? We've heard from a close personal source that you don't have anyone to take care of her."

"I'm taking care of her," Delaney says proudly. "She's my family."

Love slams into me. What I ever did to deserve her, I don't know.

What she doesn't say is that Raven and I have moved in with her, and she's quit her library job to take care of Raven on the days the nurse can't come by. Skye said she'd chip in a day a week too.

Fred looks at the viewers. "Well, the question on everyone's mind is if you'll be playing for Waylon this year."

I swallow. "I don't know. I haven't been informed yet."

He nods. "What do you think the ruling will be when it comes to being drafted?"

"I have no idea." I look at Delaney and Raven. "We're still waiting to hear."

I do know that whatever happens, I'll be okay.

Delaney comes out of the kitchen, wearing a big grin and her *May the Fork Be With You* apron. She and Raven are making dinner and pecan pie for Ryder since he helped us move into her place a few weeks back.

It's the end of the year, and we're celebrating.

I think back to how everything played out after the interview. After much discussion and interviews, it was determined that the only technical rule I broke was accepting money. There was no indication of foul play, and most importantly, no gambling. Because the scandal involved several star players in the SEC who'd been preyed upon by offerings of big money, the NCAA decided not to kick us out of college football completely. Myself, along with the other players, would be sitting out the first five games of the year.

It was enough.

It was hope.

As far as Muffin went, none of the players on the team would even talk to her anymore. Rumor has it she's transferring schools for her senior year.

This fall is going to be the year—*my year*. I look at Delaney and watch as she shows Raven how to make her Nana's pie. She catches my eye and smiles as Han weaves between their legs, meowing for a table scrap.

"I love you," I mouth at her as she straightens up. She's everything, mine, and maybe she has been since the night of the bonfire. We just had to figure it out.

She smiles, a slow blush working up her cheeks. "I know," she mouths back.

I burst out laughing.

Forget this being my year. I look at her and Raven.

This is our year.

EPILOGUE

TWO YEARS LATER

DELANEY

I wake up, and Maverick's not in bed. *That's weird.* It's not quite eight in the morning and it's the off-season, which means he gets to sleep in before training starts. Spotting the blue dress shirt he wore last night when we went out to dinner, I pick it up off the floor where I tossed it before we made love. I pull it on, pad over to the window, and look out over the Nashville skyline from our penthouse.

I sigh contentedly. After winning the national championship with the Waylon Wildcats, Maverick went on to be drafted in the first round by the Tennessee Titans. He's already broken two records, and they went to the Super Bowl this year. They were defeated, but like he says, it gives him something to work for.

I look at the picture of him and me and Raven on the nightstand and smile. Somehow we managed to juggle her and classes and football our senior year, and because Maverick was so open about the reason he fought, people came out of the woodwork to help us. Mrs. Watson from Pineview herself volunteered to donate services to Raven, including riding lessons and art classes at Pineview.

She lived with us until Maverick was drafted, and then made it clear that while she loved us, she did not want to be attached to us at the hip. So, we did some research and found her a facility nearly identical to Pineview in Nashville.

As for me, I'm designing a line of clothing for my new Geek Girl fashion label and volunteer weekly at a local animal shelter. Maverick loves coming with me too, although I don't think he'd ever admit it. Rescuing animals has become his charitable calling card, whether he meant it to or not.

I hear clanging from the living room and make my way there.

"Mav?" I call. "Where are you?"

I make my way down the hall and into the den then come to a halt at the vision I see. Standing smack dab in front of the floor-to-ceiling windows is Maverick dressed as a…Jedi?

I give him a careful once-over, taking in the white leggings with brown boots, the beige tunic with a utility belt, and the light saber holder. A brown overcoat is draped over the getup, and I rub my eyes. The detail is amazing and he looks professional, like something straight out of the movies.

"Morning, gorgeous." He strikes a pose, waving around a blue light saber that makes a *whooshing* sound with each movement.

"Morning, babe. Where did you get this outfit?" I'm impressed and starting to wonder if I can get a Princess Leia one. "Are we going to a comic con somewhere?"

"I had it made. And no, we're staying in today. Just you and me."

Cool. We've been busy these past few weeks, and it would be great to just relax at home. Maverick swings the sword and Han darts from behind a chair, paws swatting at the light saber as he runs past.

I giggle. "Nice moves. You've got Han riled up now."

I expect him to laugh with me, and he does flash me a brief smile, but there's something about his expression that's different. It's intense, as if he's about to head out to the most important football game of his life.

"What's going on? Are you okay?" I say, moving in closer.

"More than okay. It's the best day of my life," he says as he sets the light saber on a chair and kneels down in front of me. From the coffee table, he picks up a black velvet box that I hadn't noticed yet and pops it open. Inside is a ring with the biggest square cut solitaire diamond I've ever seen.

I blink. My body flutters and I can't breathe.

He gazes up at me with those steel blue eyes, the ones I hold close to my heart every night when I go to sleep.

"It feels like I've waited forever to do this. Delaney Renee Shaw, will you marry me and make me the happiest Jedi in the universe? I promise to always love you—and your cats—and give you everything you could ever want, body and soul."

Tears flood my eyes as I take him in: his pure heart, the way he fights for those he loves, the way he loves *me*.

"Yes. Always. You are everything."

"*You're* everything, Buttercup, and I couldn't have made it without you by my side." He stands up, cups my face, and kisses me, and I know that no matter what, he and I can do anything together.

THE END

I DARE YOU

YOU

RECIPES

Nana's Super Secret Pecan Pie

INGREDIENTS:

1 cup of sugar
1 ½ cups of corn syrup (half dark and half light
4 eggs
¼ cup butter
1 ½ teaspoon vanilla
1 ½ cups pecans, broken
1 unbaked deep dish pie shell

INSTRUCTIONS:
1. In saucepan, boil sugar and corn syrup together for 2 to 3 minutes and then set aside to cool.
2. In large bowl beat eggs lightly and slowly pour the syrup mixture into the eggs, stirring constantly.
3. Strain the mixture to make sure it's smooth and lump free. Stir in butter, vanilla, and pecans and pour into crust.
4. Bake in a 350°F oven for about 45 to 60 minutes or until set.

Chocolate Chip Cookies

INGREDIENTS:

8 tablespoons of salted butter
1/2 cup white sugar
1/4 cup packed light brown sugar
1 teaspoon vanilla
1 egg
1 ½ cups all purpose flour
1/2 teaspoon baking soda
1/4 teaspoon salt
3/4 cup chocolate chips

INSTRUCTIONS:

1. Preheat the oven to 350 degrees. Microwave the butter for about 40 seconds to just barely melt it. It shouldn't be hot – but it should be almost entirely in liquid form.
2. Using a stand mixer or electric beaters, beat the butter with the sugars until creamy. Add the vanilla and the egg; beat on low speed until just incorporated or so (if you beat the egg for too long, the cookies will be stiff).
3. Add the flour, baking soda, and salt. Mix until crumbles form. Use your hands to press the crumbles together into a dough. It should form one large ball that is easy to handle (right at the stage between "wet" dough and "dry" dough). Add the chocolate chips and incorporate with your hands.
4. Roll the dough into 12 large balls (or 9 for HUGELY

awesome cookies) and place on a cookie sheet. Bake for 9-11 minutes until the cookies look puffy and dry and just barely golden.

5. DO NOT OVERBAKE. This advice is probably written on every cookie recipe everywhere, but this is essential for keeping the cookies soft. Take them out even if they look like they're not done yet.

6. Let them cool on the pan for a good 30 minutes.

Double Chocolate Muffins

INGREDIENTS:

2 cups all-purpose flour
1 cup white sugar
3/4 cup chocolate chips
1/2 cup unsweetened cocoa powder
1 teaspoon baking soda
1 egg
1 cup plain yogurt
1/2 cup milk
1 teaspoon vanilla extract
1/2 cup vegetable oil
1/4 cup chocolate chips

DIRECTIONS
1. Preheat oven to 400 degrees F (200 degrees C). Grease 12 muffin cups or line with paper muffin liners.
2. Combine flour, sugar, 3/4 cup chocolate chips, cocoa powder, and baking soda in a large bowl. Whisk egg, yogurt, milk, vanilla, and vegetable oil in another bowl until smooth; pour into chocolate mixture and stir until batter is just blended. Fill prepared muffin cups 3/4 full and sprinkle with remaining 1/4 cup chocolate chips.
3. Bake in preheated oven until a toothpick inserted into the center comes out clean, about 20 minutes. Cool in the pans for 10 minutes before removing to cool completely on a wire rack.

BOOKS AND STALKING

Welcome to a detailed list of all my books PLUS the various places to stalk me, which I highly encourage.

My series books are standalones about brand new couples. All are in Kindle Unlimited at the moment. (high-fives)

Briarwood Academy Series: Angsty, heartfelt new adult stand-alone romances
Very Bad Things: http://amzn.to/2FfRNBW
Very Wicked Beginnings (Prequel): http://amzn.to/2sH6DPp
Very Wicked Things: http://amzn.to/2FifucO
Very Twisted Things: http://amzn.to/2C96hF4

British Bad Boys Series: Steamy and emotional new adult/ contemporary romance with British heroes
Dirty English: http://amzn.to/2BCPlpv
Filthy English: http://amzn.to/2Cc8ijK

The Hot Jock and the Smart Girl:
Fake Fiancée: http://amzn.to/2sHv3IG

Ex-NFL player and the Sassy Reporter
The Last Guy (w/Tia Louise): http://amzn.to/2BFmMHR

British Rock Star/Stepbrother:
Spider: http://amzn.to/2GsXX1e

Stalk Me:

➥ Website: http://www.ilsamaddenmills.com
➥ News Letter: (Free Book a Month): http://www.ilsamadden-mills.com/contact
➥ Instagram: https://www.instagram.com/ilsamaddenmills/
➥ Goodreads: http://bit.ly/2EESfM9
➥ Bookbub: http://bit.ly/2GaR6cn
➥ Amazon: http://amzn.to/2nY2pxT
➥ Book+Main: https://bookandmainbites.com/ilsamaddenmills

ABOUT THE AUTHOR

Wall Street Journal, New York Times, and *USA Today* best-selling author Ilsa Madden-Mills writes about strong heroines and sexy alpha males that sometimes you just want to slap. She's best known for her angsty, heartfelt new adult college romances.

A former high school English teacher, she adores all things Pride and Prejudice; Mr. Darcy is her ultimate hero.

She's addicted to frothy coffee beverages, Vampire Dairies, and any kind of book featuring unicorns and sword-wielding females.

Join her Unicorn Girls FB group for special excerpts, prizes, and snarky fun!
https://www.facebook.com/groups/ilsasunicorngirls/

34551921R00146

Made in the USA
Middletown, DE
26 January 2019